After All This Time

Beca Lewis

Perception Publishing

Contents

One

It didn't take Nicky Blair long to realize she couldn't remain anonymous for long in a town like Spring Falls. Not just because it was a small town. It was that the people were curious and acted friendly. She didn't know yet if the friendliness was real or fake. She had been aware for too long about the duplicity of people to accept things at face value. People often acted one way but thought and did another.

So she didn't trust them. At all.

However, despite herself, she hoped it was true—hoped that the friendliness was genuine. Still, she didn't like it. How was she supposed to watch what people were doing without them noticing, when they kept noticing her and asking her questions? Questions she didn't want to answer.

Even giving up her name was tricky. At first, she thought she might make one up. But Nicky knew herself well enough to know that she wouldn't remember a made-up name. She had so much going on inside her it was entirely possible she would say her real name by accident because she'd forgotten she was hiding who she was and why she was in Spring Falls.

So, reluctantly, she told people an edited version of what they wanted to know. It was easy because there wasn't much to tell. She was a nobody. Had been for years.

Once, a long time ago, she had a proper job, but had become bored almost immediately. So she moved around, taking odd jobs everywhere she went. She'd rent a room in someone's house, and when they got upset with her, or she with them—which would happen eventually—she'd move on.

Nicky kept no social media presence. She used the internet to get what she wanted. She didn't let it use her. It had been a lonely life. But it was what she thought she wanted.

Until she started remembering what she had been trying to forget for years, dreaming about it when asleep and startled by memories when awake. Finally, she gave in and let herself remember. All of it. At least what she knew. What she didn't know was the reason she ended up in Spring Falls.

That Spring Falls was near where the nightmare of her life had begun surprised her. She could almost hear her father say: "The world moves in mysterious ways."

She knew that to be true. However, what her father never told her, probably because he didn't know himself until it was too late, is that "mysterious" doesn't always—or often mean—in good ways.

So now, all these years later, she was in a town close to where she grew up, sitting in a tiny diner, trying to remain invisible. And failing. Everyone from the waitress to the couple sitting a few tables over said hello and smiled. It was hard not to smile back, even though she didn't want to. That they paid attention to her pissed her off. It was ruining her plan to be a nobody.

Nicky purposefully kept her hair un-styled and dyed a dirty, dark brown. When her pure white hair started showing, she covered it up. She dressed like everyone else, so her clothes didn't make her stand out from the crowd. It was impossible to hide her striking blue eyes, so when she wasn't wearing brown contact lenses she got in the habit of looking down. All in an attempt to avoid calling attention to herself.

Until Spring Falls, staying as invisible as possible had always worked. She arrived in Spring Falls a week ago and, as always, had rented a room in a home and kept to herself. However, instead of ignoring her, as most people did, her landlady was friendly and curious, like the rest of the town.

Nothing about Spring Falls was working out the way she wanted it to. However, Nicky had to admit to herself that if she wasn't here on a mission of revenge, she might like this place. It reminded her of her hometown of Jakestown before it changed. Except Jakestown was even smaller. It barely existed on the map. Nicky figured that they probably named it after some guy named Jake who first homesteaded the place.

Nicky had known it was a good place to grow up, even when she resented it. Everyone seemed content with their tiny farming town, even though there was the constant smell of animals when the wind drifted in a certain way, and every few years the crop would fail because of the weather or a swarm of insects devoured them before harvest time.

The men would gather at the diner on the main street for breakfast, and if it was too wet to plant or harvest, almost every man in town could be found there, drinking one cup of coffee after another, talking about whatever men talked about.

The women of Jakestown did church socials and gathered in living rooms to discuss the day, children, and the town's needs, as they quilted or knitted. Because, as her mother always said, men talked about nothing for hours while women talked about what counted and kept on working. The women helped each other with kids, dinners, and chores if someone got sick.

Jakestown was a pleasant place, but Nicky had always wanted more. She wanted to be someone different. Who that someone would be, Nicky hadn't known. All that Nicky knew then was she wanted to change her life and be on her own. So she left home as soon as possible, traveling a little, trying to discover her place in the world.

But then Sara went missing. And Nicky's life changed, as did the life of everyone in Jakestown. When it became clear that Sara would never be coming back, that something terrible had happened, the town's happiness switched off. Each year that Sara stayed missing, the town died a little more.

Before she stopped visiting, Nicky thought the town gave off a smell of decay that drove people away. No one moved there. People left. Distrust settled like dust on people's hearts.

The thought "it could be any of us" lingered unspoken, everyone afraid to think that it could have been their neighbor that made Sara disappear. Open doors closed, and the joy that was Jakestown faded away.

Nicky stopped going home a few years after Sara went missing. Visiting her parents while they were alive was like visiting when they were dead, except for the tears. Because when they were alive, the tears never stopped as they searched and searched for the daughter they loved. So many tears you'd think they would wash away their house.

Instead, the tears washed away her parents, who now lay side by side in a graveyard in Jakestown. For all Nicky knew, they were still crying. Not her. She didn't cry then and she didn't cry now.

Nicky knew that someday it would all catch up with her, and perhaps her tears would wash her away too, but right now, she was on a mission, and tears would only get in the way. Now she was an avenging angel, dark and distrustful. She would finally find out what happened to her sister, no matter the cost to herself.

And Nicky believed the answer was in this town called Spring Falls. If it was, then all hell was going to break loose. But first, she had to be sure. Then she would do what needed to be done to punish the person who took her sister away from her and drowned her parents in their tears.

Two

That evening, Nicky found two of the people she was stalking sitting in the back of the room where the lights were dim, hoping no one they knew would see them. But if someone was looking their way, they were hard to miss, and Nicky—who always scanned a room before entering—paused for a moment to study the woman with the soft red hair and the man with blond hair going gray.

They fascinated Nicky. They were young and old at the same time. Nicky couldn't keep herself from liking them, wanting to know more about them, how they felt about each other, and how they were doing. She felt as if they were part of her story, too. Or she hoped they would be. But she didn't want to talk to them, not yet. They were in their own world, and she didn't want to disturb them. Besides, she wasn't ready—yet.

This room smells of secrets, Nicky thought. *Or maybe it's me that smells because I am a bundle of secrets.*

Looking around the room, Nicky saw families, couples, and even a teenage boy and girl who could barely look at each other. Nicky thought they were probably out on their first date. A flash of memory went by of her and her first date. Lifetimes ago when the future looked bright, and anything had been possible. Now everything in her life had narrowed down from a life of possibilities to one simple focus. Find out what happened to Sara.

The restaurant was dark but clean, and Nicky thought she might actually find something here that she felt like eating. So she settled herself down at a small table in another dark corner of the restaurant, hoping she was right about the food.

The table was sticky, and the waitress had to wipe it down with a rag before she could set down the glass of water for Nicky. Nicky smiled at the waitress as she handed Nicky a menu and then asked her to wait there for a sec because she wanted to order immediately. Nicky pointed to two choices on the menu, asked the waitress what she would order, and then took her advice, along with a diet soda, whatever they had.

While Nicky ate her pasta—which she was delighted to discover was as delicious as the waitress said it would be—she casually glanced at the other tables, lingering only briefly on the two people she had seen and admired. They wouldn't have noticed her anyway. They were busy laughing and discussing something that seemed to please them. Once in a while, they took bites of food as if they had just remembered that was why they were there.

They look harmless enough, Nicky said to herself, while admitting that it was often the harmless ones that hurt the most. She hoped these two would be what she needed. She wanted them to help her find the person who needed to be stopped and punished.

But for now, she would be an observer and not a participant. Because first she had to know if she could trust them.

Nicky had read about the two of them on the internet. Judith Zoe practically ran the town of Spring Falls, but behind the scenes. She and the people she hired did the bookkeeping and accounting for many of the town's businesses. Plus, Judith had a reputation for speaking up loudly whenever things were wrong. At least wrong, in Judith's opinion.

After researching what Judith felt was wrong, Nicky had to admit she agreed with most of her conclusions. Which was why she hoped Judith was who she appeared to be. She would be a necessary part of Nicky's plan if she was.

The man lived a few hours away, but Nicky suspected he was thinking of moving his estate planning practice to Spring Falls. Because of Judith. In the meantime, they seemed to want to keep their relationship quiet, which was why they were hiding in the back of a dim restaurant in the next town over from Spring Falls.

Nicky had no desire to out their secret, although Nicky suspected that more people knew about them than they expected. Perhaps the two of them were the only people who were hiding from the truth. Hiding it from themselves. Nicky understood that. She had hidden away from wanting to know the truth for years.

Then one day, the part of her that was running and hiding said that was enough. It was time for justice. And that day, she started moving towards the answers instead of running.

And now, she was ready to punish the man who hurt her sister. But first, she would need to be sure she had the right person. Which meant she had to make a few friends. Or pretend to anyway. Nicky thought she'd start with the woman with red hair.

Three

Cindy Lee Jones glanced at her phone lying on the counter and realized she had just a few minutes before she was supposed to meet Judith at the coffee shop for their regular Monday morning chat.

Even though all of the Ruby Sisters had returned to Spring Falls, and they could have included them in their Monday morning coffees, they didn't. After all the years when it was just the two of them, they had built a habit they both wanted to keep.

Cindy was grateful. She needed alone time with Judith to talk things through. Judith always saw things logically, while Cindy often lived in a sea of emotions.

Besides, Cindy knew Judith had been out of town for a few days and was looking forward to hearing where she had gone—if she could worm it out of her. There were a few things Judith had been keeping secret from everyone, or she thought she was, anyway. Cindy smiled. She'd keep Judith's secret if that's what she wanted.

As always, before going out the door, Cindy stopped in front of the hall mirror to assure herself that she was put together well enough to be seen in public. Because now that she had taken up painting again, Cindy had to make sure she didn't have paint in her hair or on her face, which she almost always did. She was a messy painter.

Cindy told herself she was only painting for something to do. She knew her paintings weren't good enough to be seen by anyone yet. Maybe never. And for sure, they would not be hanging in her art gallery where she curated and sold real art by genuine artists.

She had started the art gallery because she loved art and once believed she was an artist. Then she learned she was not. Cindy knew enough not to say that out loud to her friend Bree because Bree would give her a talking to. Bree believed that if you wanted to be something, it was because it was already part of you, and all you had to do was find that part and bring it out.

"After all," Bree would say, "I wanted to be a writer, and now look, I am."

Cindy snorted to herself, thinking, *yea right*. She knew many disillusioned people who thought they could be something but never made it. It didn't always work out how Bree claimed it would. Besides, Cindy knew that although Bree worked hard at being a writer, she wasn't acknowledging a certain amount of luck that got her where she was now—a famous spicy romance writer using the pen name of R.B. Curtis.

And although it was sad Bree lost her husband, Bree was now a mother and grandmother, and Bree didn't make that happen either. It happened to her, and the Ruby Sisters and Bree's dead husband were the ones that made sure Bree ended up the happy camper she was right now.

To herself, Cindy had to admit she felt a certain amount of resentment towards Bree, and she knew it was irrational. Although, yes, she was the one who had offered to help Bree after her husband died, and she could have said no. She could have chosen not to go to rescue her. But she did. She had loved it. And when she wasn't feeling grumpy, she had to admit she loved every minute in her makeshift studio pretending to be an artist.

Besides, she and Bree had been best friends forever. And it was because of Bree that she survived school. It was Bree who stretched out her hand to her in first grade. So it was only fitting that she had reached out to Bree when she needed help.

Cindy wrapped a soft blue scarf around her neck, fluffed her blond hair—now shorter and streaked with gray—glared at herself in the mirror, and told herself to stop it. Being happy for other people's happiness was a part of who she was. Besides, in the aftermath of it all, she ended up with one of her best friends helping her with her business and another living with her until she found a place of her own.

As she grabbed her purse and keys off the kitchen counter, she called up to Marsha, "I'm off," and heard a faint answer of "Have a great day!"

"I will! You too!" Cindy said, and smiled to herself. She knew she would because she would choose to. Because, despite sometimes being miffed at Bree and her beliefs, she had adopted a few of them for herself.

Besides, having coffee with Judith was always enlightening and entertaining. And then, after coffee, she, Janet, and Mimi would be busy with customers and Internet art orders at her gallery for the rest of the day. Life was good, and her whiny self would not spoil the day for her or anyone else.

Upstairs, Marsha Melinda Martin groaned and rolled over in bed, telling herself to get up, but not having any luck convincing herself to do so. If she was a good houseguest, she would have been up before Cindy and made coffee and maybe breakfast for her. Then she'd tidy up the house before doing something with her day.

But she was not a good houseguest, and she and Cindy both knew it. Cindy said nothing other than that she was happy to have the company. But Marsha couldn't believe that was entirely true. After all, she had been there for months when it was meant to be a few days—at the most, a week or two—while she decided what to do with herself.

Paul's letter to everyone after he died begging them to help his wife recover her life had been a catalyst for all of them. Except for her. Everyone else was moving on with their lives, while she wasted time lying in bed or reading books in the soft chair in the living room with the curtains closed. Keeping the real world out.

Because, after years of first trying to make it on Broadway in New York, where she was only modestly successful, and then running a dance school, she had run out of a desire to do anything.

Marsha knew that selling her school and moving to Spring Falls was probably the right move for her, but now what? She was no closer to knowing what to do with herself than she was months ago when Cindy invited her to stay with her.

Something had to change. Inactivity and boredom were not something she had ever indulged in before and she had to stop it now.

Maybe tomorrow, Marsha mumbled to herself as she rolled over, pulled the covers around her, and went back to sleep.

Four

April May Zane Page stared at the house her husband Ron bought for her and asked herself why. Why did he think she would want this monstrosity of a house?

When she asked for a house, she had been thinking of a small two-bedroom home where they would sit by the fire at night in the winter and talk over their day together. Perhaps in the summer, they would step out onto a lovely porch and watch the town walk by.

That's what she had asked him to get her—a house in town where she could be part of the community and could walk to work at the art gallery if she wanted to.

But this? This was a monster of a house. Two stories, five bedrooms, three baths. It was the biggest house Ron could find that fulfilled the one criteria she had said was non-negotiable. She wanted to be able to walk to work. What Ron managed to do was buy the one place in town that, to her, stood out like a sore thumb. Much too big for a cozy town.

April sighed. Ron had supplied what she had asked for, and she couldn't fault him for wanting to make a good impression. Being seen as successful was important to him, and she wanted him to be happy. Especially now, because she felt as if she was finally coming into her own. And if he was happy, it meant she had more freedom for herself.

Working at Cindy's art gallery brought her more pleasure than she could have imagined and it was sparking ideas for what she wanted to do—maybe as an artist herself. As April stared at the house, trying to love it, it occurred to her that perhaps Ron was right. She might need a bigger house. Maybe she could use one bedroom for a studio, and they would still have extra bedrooms in case their two children wanted to come visit.

Smiling at that thought, April reached out and held her husband's hand, trying to feel the joy that he wanted her to feel for his gift to her.

As if he could hear her thoughts, Ron said, "I know it's bigger than you wanted, but I had to get the best for you. I'm sure you will make it into something perfect for the two of us."

April turned to look at her husband. They were standing on the lawn that would be green in the summer, but was now covered in a thin layer of snow. They stood underneath a massive red maple, leafless at the moment. April loved this tree, even leafless, so she decided if she loved the tree, she could love the house.

Besides, she loved her husband, and he was only trying to make up for losing his temper the day he threw everything out of the refrigerator onto the floor. She had been terrified and fled back home to Spring Falls.

Her decision to stay had upset Ron at first, but she was grateful that he was willing to move with her and they weren't fighting anymore about her decision. However, they had also kept their other house in Silver Lake. A housekeeper came once a week to clean it, and a landscaper came every few weeks to maintain its look. She had complained about how much that cost. Why not sell it?

Ron said no, he had the money to keep it up. Besides, he could stay there while he worked, and they had left it at that. Looking at how huge the house was they now owned in Spring Falls, April was afraid to ask how much this house cost and how much it would cost to maintain it. She couldn't do it by herself. And she didn't want to either.

Once again, Ron must have known what she was thinking because he said he had already hired a housekeeper and landscape company for her. All she had to do was tell them what she wanted. And he had contractors standing by, waiting for her instructions to fix or change anything she wanted in the house.

How can I not love him for this? April thought. She stood on her tiptoes and kissed him, then leaning into his chest, his arms around her, she said thank you, and meant it, as visions of what she could do to this massive house to make it welcoming to everyone started forming in her head.

April's phone beeped, telling her she had a message, but she ignored it. She knew that Ron wanted her full attention when she was with him. She had always known that, even though for years she had thought nothing about it. Until her friends commented on it.

"Well, it's kind of controlling," her friend Judith had said when April had told her why she never responded right away to texts and calls when she was with Ron.

"It's just a small thing," April had answered. "It keeps him happy, and since he isn't in town for long periods of time, it seems like a simple thing to do to keep him happy."

Judith had mumbled in response and let it go. But April knew it was only because Judith was her friend that Judith both worried and let it go. It had been Judith who had talked her up off the floor after Ron's temper explosion, and got her to Spring Falls.

And then all the Ruby Sisters arrived, and she felt safe and loved again, just as she had with them all throughout their years growing up together.

Now they were long past grown up, and were sliding into the other side of life, having passed the big divide between young and getting old. For years the five of them had been apart, and now they were back together again thanks to Bree's husband leaving a letter for all of them that they received after he died.

His last gift to all of them was to unite them, but to his wife Bree, he had given the best gift of all. He had led her back to her daughter, Mary, who Bree had given up for adoption twenty-eight years before. Now Bree had a grandchild and all the Ruby Sisters were the child's aunts.

Thank you, Paul, April whispered just in case he could still hear her.

Suddenly, April knew why her phone had beeped. It wasn't a phone call. It was a reminder that today was the day she had promised Bree she would come over and watch little Rhoberta Nora Patterson while Bree met with her agent. Bree's daughter Mary had gone back to work, but now only worked at the restaurant at lunch so she could be home at night, and Bree babysat while she worked.

Once again, Ron knew what she was thinking. He glanced at his watch, and said, "Hey, aren't you supposed to be at Bree's? Want me to drive you there?"

A few minutes later, April leaned over and kissed her husband before sliding out of the car. She turned and waved and then wondered if she had told him she was babysitting that day. She hadn't thought she had, so how had he known? She shrugged it away as a memory lapse on her part.

Ron waved back and smiled to himself, thinking that April was still as beautiful as the day he met her. He was such a lucky man. He would do whatever it took to make her happy, because she was his forever, and he really couldn't live without her.

Five

Ron stayed in the car outside of Bree's home until he saw Bree, holding the baby against her shoulder, open the door and let April in.

Behind her, Ron could see the clean, open hallway. Knowing Bree, he knew her entire house looked that way. It was one thing he appreciated about her. Everything in its place. Nothing wasted or useless. He liked that. He tried to live with that idea in mind himself.

Bree waved, and he waved back with a smile, appreciating that Bree was trying to be friends again. Ron knew that all of April's friends were making an effort to be friendly to him, and he was doing everything he could to give them reasons to trust him, as they once did.

When Ron first met the women who had made a pact together in elementary school and then named themselves the Ruby Sisters, they had been as charmed and delighted by him as he was with them.

But it had been April who stole his heart the moment he sat beside her in history class at the community college.

From the moment he saw her, he was hers, and she was his. It had taken him by surprise that he could care so much about someone. Even though they both had only been nineteen, Ron had already planned out a life for himself. He would become wealthy and powerful. Not necessarily famous. The type of wealth he wanted would be quiet and private.

And although he knew he would have a wife—because that would be expected of him—he didn't know he would love her so much. The children were an afterthought, and if he was being honest with himself, he loved that they had lives of their own now and lived far enough away that they would only see them from time to time.

April had been enough for him for his entire adult life and he had almost blown it all with one mistake.

Now he had but one focus, to have April fully trust him again. That meant he also had to recapture the trust of the Ruby Sisters. He knew he had screwed up by getting mad at April last spring when all she had wanted to do was help Bree after her husband Paul's death. But he hadn't been really listening as she prattled on and on about Judith and Bree and Paul's letter.

He only really heard her when she said she was going to Spring Falls to join the Ruby Sisters in helping Bree, as Paul requested in his letter. As her words sunk in, they felt like a stab to his heart, and his first thought was that April was not choosing him first and that meant he was losing her.

And he had lost control. At home. In front of April. He could barely think about it now, knowing what it might have cost him. And it hadn't been her fault it had happened either. It was entirely his fault that he lost control, especially over such a minor thing.

It was simply the wrong day to stand up to him, otherwise it would have been just an ordinary discussion. He would have explained how going to Spring Falls wasn't a good idea, and April would have listened as she always did because she understood they belonged to each other and chose each other first. He needed her at home in order to function well in his business. And it was his business that gave her everything she ever desired.

However, that morning, while she prattled on, he had been thinking about the client who informed him the day before that he was moving his investment money to another firm. He had let that feeling of betrayal upset him and had spent the entire night barely sleeping, thinking of ways to dissuade the client from transferring his funds. Then April had asked the wrong question at the wrong time.

After his temper tantrum at home, laying waste to the contents of the refrigerator, he had gone to the office and pulled himself together. By the end of the day and after a few well-placed phone calls, the client had changed his mind. And he had forgotten the whole nasty business at home.

Returning home after work and not finding April there was shocking. And it woke him up. He had been complacent. Everything in his life and business had been going so well for so long, he had forgotten how easily things could fall apart with one minor mistake.

That tantrum had cost him more than April would ever know. But he had moved quickly to fix it. Finding April in Spring Falls, he apologized, and she accepted—with a few conditions. She wanted to work at Bree's art gallery, she wanted to live in Spring Falls, and she wanted to walk to work.

He agreed to all of it, even though he was worried about what would happen when they returned to Spring Falls. But all his worries fell away when nothing terrible happened. Although her friends had given him the cold shoulder at first, he knew they would eventually forgive him for his outburst. If only for April's sake, which was fine with him.

All he needed was for them to accept him enough so he could rebuild his life with April. He would do whatever it took to make sure April was happy and their unit of two would stay together.

However, the move to Spring Falls meant he had to think of how to continue to run his business in Silver Lake.

April believed he worked for someone else. She, like most people, didn't know that he was the owner of the business, and he wanted it to stay that way. It gave him greater leverage, being the power behind the business rather than the face of it. Since April didn't know he was the boss, she believed he had to stay in Silver Lake sometimes in order to keep his job, which meant it made sense to keep their house there. It gave him a place to stay while seeing clients at the office.

Yes, at first he had disliked the arrangement that April had forced him to make. But it didn't take long to see the advantages of letting April stay in Spring Falls and buying her the house she deserved there. Because now he had a private home all to himself in Silver Lake.

April said she had no interest in returning to Silver Lake, so he had done what she asked. He had moved all their furniture to the new home in Spring Falls. He kept only what he needed for himself. Now that everything was settling down, April's decision to move was turning out to be a fantastic stroke of luck for him.

Before pulling away from the house, Ron glanced in the rear-view mirror and saw the handsome man he had become reflected back at him, and smiled at his good fortune.

Sometimes you need to let go to have good things happen, Ron said to himself. He expected more to come his way, but first he had some plans to make.

Six

B y the time Bree turned from locking the door, April had removed her coat and shoes and was reaching out for the baby.

"I've been looking forward to spending a little time with this sweet one," she said as she snuggled into the neck of month-old little Rho, breathing in the baby smell and feeling all her worries fade away.

She would have loved Mary's baby even if she hadn't turned out to be Bree's grandchild. They all would have, because Mary Patterson had become part of their world before the big reveal that she was the daughter Bree had given away.

When the Ruby Sisters discovered that Bree and Paul had left Spring Falls and disappeared from their lives because Bree didn't want them to know she was pregnant, or more to the point, why she was pregnant, they were all heartbroken and angry. Didn't Bree know that she could have turned to them for help? They would have stood by her, they would have understood.

Even now, after all the healing that had taken place, Bree remained silent about Mary's father. She said some secrets must remain secret, and who Mary's father was had to be one of those secrets. Except now that Mary had taken a DNA test to find her parents—which is how she found Bree—all of them felt as if it was only a matter of time until Mary's father and the secret was revealed.

April wondered if Bree had thought that through, and decided that the ever logical Bree must have. *But then everyone turns a blind eye to the inevitable once in a while, even Bree*, April thought to herself.

"Thanks for watching her, April. I made coffee for you, and Judith dropped off some of her famous cinnamon buns. It's all in the kitchen. I'll be in my office for about an hour. And Mary left some milk for Rho in case she gets hungry again."

"Take your time. Cindy isn't expecting me at the gallery today. So I am all yours, and Rho's."

Before Bree stepped into her office, she turned back to look at April and Rho and wondered why she had ever thought they wouldn't accept her after what happened. But that was all over now. They were all safe and together in Spring Falls. Now all she had to do was convince her agent she knew what she was doing.

April smiled back at Bree, giving her a thumbs up and holding Rho against her shoulder, went into the kitchen to get the promised treats. She loved being in Bree's home. It was not full of stuff. Partially because Bree was starting over, but also it was how Bree liked things. Simple, uncluttered, and comfortable. Bree had kept the house colors muted with dark green and blue hues that blended well with the dove gray walls and polished wood floors.

After getting a coffee and a cinnamon bun, April returned to the living room and settled into one of the large comfortable chairs, slipped off her shoes, and let her feet sink into the plush and thick throw rug that sat between the couch and the chairs. Bree had planned everything for comfort but also safety for when Rho started to walk, with rounded corners on everything. April knew if she looked all the wall sockets would be covered. She already knew the drawers and cupboards were baby proof. *Almost April proof,* she laughed to herself. It had taken her a minute to figure out how the drawer worked the first time she came over.

A gas fireplace glowed beneath a large TV screen. Last week, all the Ruby Sisters came over to watch a movie with Bree, eating popcorn, feet propped up on the large coffee table in front of the couch. Even Bree's feet were on the table, something she would not think of doing any other day.

The house was small, solid, and quiet. Small enough for Bree, but comfortable for when the Ruby Sisters came to visit. Just the kind of house she had wanted. Not the large one Ron had bought for her.

Bree's office was at the end of the house, facing out to a small garden, the same garden that the kitchen dining room area also opened up to. It was too cold to eat out there now, but they had roasted marshmallows over a fire one night right after Rho was born.

Snuggling into the lush chair that rocked, April patted Rho's back. She could see the wind whipping around the trees outside the large window that faced the street. The sky had become a dark gray. Snow was on the way. She closed her eyes and let herself relax and daydream about how she could make her large, overbearing house feel like this.

Less than an hour later, Bree returned, smiling at the sight of April and Rho asleep in the chair. It was something she had never dreamed she would see, and tears formed in her eyes. Slipping away into the kitchen, she poured herself a cup of coffee and took another cinnamon bun.

It was a day of celebration. And besides, she was still trying to put back on some of the weight she had lost after Paul's death. It made her happy that now when she looked in a mirror she was beginning to look like herself again. Not the ghost woman she had felt like before returning to Spring Falls.

In the living room, April opened her eyes as Bree came in with her coffee and cinnamon bun. Seeing the smile on Bree's face, she asked, "Your agent agreed?"

"She did. I'll write under my own name from now on. And they are willing for me to take my time to find a new voice for myself. I thought I didn't care, but when she said yes, and that all the people that worked on my books before would be working on the new ones, I realized how much I wanted that to happen."

"It's like that sometimes, isn't it?" April said down at Rho, who remained sound asleep in her arms.

"You feel that way about coming back here, don't you?"

April nodded. "I didn't know how much I wanted to return until I was here, and with all of you. And I'm glad that Ron is happy with the arrangement, too."

Bree nodded, feeling her stomach clench at the mention of Ron. But her friend loved him, and there was no value in telling her what she knew about him. That was in the past. He had changed. She was sure of that because it had to be that way for all of them.

But as Bree watched April snuggle with Rho, she wondered how long she planned on fooling herself. *As long as it takes*, she told herself.

Seven

As Judith sat in the coffee shop waiting for Cindy, she thought about last night's dinner with Bruce.

She had seen the woman sitting in the corner watching them, but she hadn't mentioned it to Bruce. He had driven a few hours to see her, and she decided not to spoil it by bringing up her suspicions.

However, something about the woman had made her uneasy. She was sure the woman had been spying on them. But why? Judith didn't think the woman was dangerous, but she wanted something, and that meant she would need to find out what it was as soon as possible.

But yesterday, she had turned away from the woman and focused her attention on Bruce because he had just told her he was thinking of moving to Spring Falls.

He said he liked it there. It was big enough to support a small estate planning practice. He wanted her help in selling his old practice and setting up a new one in Spring Falls.

"Are you sure you want to do that, Bruce?" Judith had asked him in various ways, hoping to trip him up so he would decide not to move. But the more she tried to make him change his mind, the more sure he became.

Judith knew he knew what she was doing. She was trying to stop whatever was happening between them. Or at least trying to make sure that if it happened, it was what they both really wanted.

She knew that if he moved to Spring Falls, it would openly state what was happening between them, and then what? However, she couldn't deny how much she liked him, how much she enjoyed their conversations that happened more and more often. Sometimes they talked on the phone, sometimes on Zoom,

And yesterday, for the second time, in person.

The first time they had met in person was when Bruce had driven in for Rho's birth, surprising them all, but especially Judith. Bruce said he had come because he had become attached to all of them while helping them work out Paul's gift. But even then, they both knew it was more than that.

Later, she learned Bruce had bought many of the things Mary and Seth needed for the baby. Judith had listened to Mary gush over Bruce's generosity and felt her heart thud in her chest. She was both terrified that it was all an act, and hoping it wasn't.

So far, though, as hard as she had tried, she hadn't been able to trip him up, and he had taken all her challenges in stride. Which made her happy and terrified her at the same time. If this kept up, someday she would have to tell him a very private thing about herself. And if he moved to Spring Falls, it would force her hand, and she didn't like that at all.

When Cindy pulled up outside the coffee shop, she could see Judith staring at her coffee cup and laughed a little to herself. She suspected Judith had been seeing Bruce, and the look on her face seemed to confirm it. It worried her. Why would Judith be resisting Bruce?

But as soon as the door opened, Judith looked up and smiled at Cindy as if nothing was on her mind. Still, Cindy decided, she would not let Judith off the hook that easily. After getting coffee, Cindy settled herself at the table.

Judith pointed to the cinnamon bun sitting on a plate and said, "I took a few over to Bree's this morning for her and April, and thought you might like one too."

"Yum, oh yes! So you were baking recently?" Cindy asked with a giggle in her voice.

Everyone knew Judith baked when she was trying to figure something out.

"Busted," Judith said, laughing.

"What's going on?"

"There's a new woman in town. It seems like everywhere I go, she's there. Do you know who I mean?"

"That's it? No other reason?"

"Well. Yes. Bruce. But I truly don't want to talk about him."

"You know he is a good guy, don't you?"

Judith nodded, but didn't answer.

Cindy smiled at her friend, thinking that Bree's husband Paul might have planned one more gift for the Ruby Sisters. Perhaps he had used Bruce as his attorney, the one that would deal with each of them, because he knew that Judith and Bruce would like each other.

Cindy wouldn't have put it past Paul. He had spent a lot of time and effort making sure Bree and her friends were happy after he was gone. Cindy knew that all of them often whispered "thank you" to Paul, just in case he was listening.

Cindy didn't believe in ghosts, but Paul's presence felt so real sometimes she would swear he was there. She hoped it was his choice. She had heard that sometimes people stay around until everyone is settled and taken care of. If he was still here, there were still things to be resolved. She knew of a few. Maybe there were more.

"What are you thinking about, Cindy?"

"Paul."

Judith nodded. "I think about him, too. Good man, after all, wasn't he?"

"Yes. Like Bruce."

Judith laughed, and said, "Yes, like Bruce. But I still don't want to talk about him right now. I want to talk about this woman. Do you know who I mean?"

"Not really. But then if she hasn't come into the gallery, I probably wouldn't have seen her. What does she look like?"

"Deliberately plain. Which makes her stand out."

"To you, Judith. For the rest of us, she probably disappears from view. Do you think that is what she is trying to do."

"I do. And yet, I think she wants me to notice, as if she has something she wants to ask me. Or find out."

"Maybe she is trying to figure out if you are a good guy."

Judith laughed. "That could be it. But I think it's time for me to find out more about her. Would you keep an eye out for her and ask Marsha too?"

"Sure, if Marsha ever decides to get herself moving again. She is really stuck. We might have to butt in soon."

"Well, maybe the mystery of this woman will give her something to do."

"What does she look like?"

"Hum. Probably in her late fifties, maybe older? Average height. Dyed dark brown un-styled hair. Clothes that look like they could be from a thrift shop. None of which suits her. I think she thinks it's a disguise. I am looking forward to disabusing her of that notion. Assuming, of course, she wants to talk."

Cindy looked around the coffee shop. "She's not here now, though."

"No, but she was walking by right before you came in."

Cindy stopped smiling and leaned forward. "Are you sure you are safe from her?"

"Not sure. Which is why I would like to find out who she is before I confront her."

"Don't do any confronting on your own," Cindy said, knowing she would do it, anyway. "Let me ask Janet and Mimi. And ask Mary. Perhaps that woman has been in the restaurant. And yes, I'll get Marsha on it. Maybe it will snap her out of her funk."

"I think this is about the Ruby Sisters. I'm not sure why I think that. It just feels that way."

Cindy leaned back in her chair and looked at her friend. Judith, the warrior queen, just as she was when they were growing up together. It wasn't just her height, or her red hair, it was who she had always been. Now, though, Judith had years of experience at fighting for what was right, so Cindy almost felt sorry for the woman Judith was looking for.

Cindy didn't have to tell Judith how much she loved and admired her. Judith would not like to hear it that way, anyway. But she knew. Just as Cindy knew that Judith loved all of them, too. And as they had before, they would work together to find out what the mystery woman wanted. Maybe nothing. But still, they had to know.

Eight

After passing by the coffee shop, Nicky kept walking, trying not to change her pace. She'd been seen, but that didn't mean she had to acknowledge it. Which shouldn't matter, since she was a nobody. But it was the way she was seen that made Nicky anxious. She had thought that Judith had noticed her at the restaurant, and now she was stupid enough to walk by her again so soon.

Sometimes you are such an idiot, she said to herself. It was a familiar refrain in her head.

When she was growing up, that voice in her head was just a bother, but after Sara went missing, it became the only thing she heard some days.

It's all your fault. If you would have stayed home instead of going off to find your way in the world, it wouldn't have happened.

Instead, she wanted to be somebody, so she ignored her sister's and parents' pleas to stay home, at least until Sara graduated from high school.

But no, that voice said, *you thought you were more important than your family, didn't you? It's all your fault.*

Nicky turned the corner into the alley that ran beside the coffee shop and crouched down, leaning against the brick wall. She put her head between her knees, trying to get her breath back, thinking she couldn't allow this to happen. Nicky knew enough to know that listening to that voice was destructive. She'd never get her revenge by punishing herself. Besides, when she was thinking logically, Nicky knew it wouldn't have made a difference if she had been there or not.

Sara had been a headstrong teenager. She did what she wanted to, when she wanted to. And because she was so beautiful and charming and sweet—when she wanted to be—she got away with it. Even with Nicky. She knew when Sara was playing her, and she let her.

Why not let her have her fun while she can, she had thought.

So everyone looked away when Sara would lie about where she was and what she was doing. Which meant she got more and more brazen about it. By the time she turned fifteen, she was climbing out of her bedroom window to see friends. Nicky knew about it. Her parents didn't.

She had kept Sara's secret, thinking it was the sisterly loving thing to do. Again. What could it hurt? But it was that lack of judgment on her part that fed her guilt. What if she had said something? Would it have made a difference?

But Nicky knew blaming herself or her sister for what happened to her would never bring her back, would never help her find who had done something to her. First, she had to prove that something had happened. Then she had to prove that the man she suspected had done it. Or maybe it was the other way around. Either way, she had to be strong, not weak, to find out what happened.

Nicky's breath calmed, and she took a deep breath and wished she hadn't. The alley looked clean enough, but it smelled like smoke and piss. She stood, keeping her hand on the wall until she was sure her legs would hold her, before returning to the sidewalk.

As she walked, Nicky thought about her sister and how no one really knew what had happened to her. Her beautiful sister, with her long blond hair and bright blue eyes, had simply disappeared.

Because of Sara's headstrong ways, no one had worried at first when she didn't come home from school. She was probably hanging out with friends. But when hours went by, and the streetlights had come on, her parents started looking. Multiple phone calls didn't turn up anything. Her friends said she had left during lunch break and they didn't see her come back.

Sneaking out at lunch was something they weren't supposed to do, but everyone did anyway. Later, when Nicky had gone home to help look for Sara, she had gone to the diner they often snuck off to. The place had huge dill pickles in a jar, and she and her friends would get one and share it along with a burger with everything on it. Much better than the food in the cafeteria or what they could pack from home.

John, the owner, had remembered that Sara was there. At least, he thought she was. After all, the group of them would be there at least once a week. He knew they were supposed to be in school. But what was he supposed to do, call the sheriff?

Besides, John had grown up in Jakestown and he, too, had snuck over to the very same diner. Later, when he realized he didn't want to leave town, John worked there, until one day the owner sold it to him. The sheriff had grown up in Jakestown, too. And like the diner's owner, had often skipped out on school. He had thought nothing of Sara skipping school to be there. It was just something they all did as they grew up.

The day Sara went missing, John said he thought she was with some boy he didn't recognize. And since he thought he knew everyone from town, he figured the boy was from another town, or passing through with his family.

The sheriff had looked at John as if he was crazy. Someone passing through here long enough to stop at the diner? No one believed that scenario. So they checked the other small towns nearby, but of course no one knew who the boy had been. And no, there were no other missing teenagers, so she hadn't run away with anyone else.

After a few months of limited searching, the town stopped. They gave up. The safety of a small, closely knit community had ended.

Even Nicky stopped looking. She couldn't stand her parents' tears or the overwhelming guilt she felt. That had started her wandering, and she had never stopped moving. Until now.

But what she was going to do was still in question. Perhaps, if Judith saw her, and was curious about her, maybe that was a good thing. She could use it to her advantage. Nicky wasn't exactly sure how to approach Judith, but if Judith came to her, it might make it easier.

As if any of this was going to be easy, Nicky thought.

All she had was a wild, hair-brained idea. She might be wrong. On the other hand, she could be right, and since she had nowhere else to go, and no one that cared about her, she had nothing to lose. Everything she loved or wanted had disappeared with Sara. And she wanted it back.

Nine

Now that there was no other choice, April got busy with her new house. She was still living at Judith's house when Ron wasn't in town. When he was, he rented a suite for them at the hotel. Although it seemed excessive to her, she knew it was Ron's way of saying he loved her, so she let herself enjoy it.

But now that the house was hers, it was time to move out of Judith's. Judith never complained, but April knew she liked her private space. It wouldn't take long to make parts of her new home livable while she fixed up the rest. Not that anything really needed to be fixed. It was beautiful how it was, but it wasn't hers. And she loved the process of designing things.

The furniture that Ron had moved from their house in Silver Lake only took up a small amount of space and now that she had seen it inside the house, she wasn't sure that it fit there, anyway. As she imagined herself in the house, April realized that once again, Ron had given her something she hadn't known she wanted. He had given her a canvas for her to design. All hers, to do as she wished.

Mary had dropped her off downtown after picking up Rho from Bree's because even though she wasn't working that day, April wanted to stop in at the gallery to say hello. Everything about the gallery inspired her.

Besides, she would rather use the gallery's office to make phone calls instead of being alone at Judith's. Since returning to Spring Falls, April had rediscovered her love of being around other people. Why she had let herself become so isolated in Silver Lake was a mystery to her.

On the way to the gallery, she glimpsed herself in a store window and smiled. She looked so different from what she had looked like when she returned to Spring Falls. Janet and Mimi had set her up with new clothes and a new hairstyle, and she had kept it up.

April giggled, realizing that Janet and Mimi had redesigned her, and now she would do that for her house.

The love of design was another thing she had forgotten about herself while living in Silver Lake. She barely had time to fix up their house in Silver Lake before their first child was born, and from there, it had been a whirlwind of parenting. There had been no time to think about what she wanted.

Once that part of her life was over, it had been too late to care about anything for herself. At least, that was what she had thought until Ron's tantrum forced her to leave home that day.

There had been no sign of his temper since then, for which she was extremely grateful. She didn't want a terrible temper to be part of who he was. She had seen him that angry only once before. But it hadn't been directed at her, so she had not been afraid for herself. The person on the other end of the phone might have been, though.

It had been years before, and Ron had left the door to his office open a crack. That was unusual. He always kept it closed when he was home working. So she had paused in the hallway, thinking of closing it for him, but as she heard him screaming on the phone she had scurried away, so he wouldn't be embarrassed about her overhearing him.

Later, at dinner, he was fine, so she never brought it up, figuring it was about something about work and she wouldn't understand, anyway.

When they were first married, she would often ask him about his work, but as time went by, she understood less and less about what he was talking about. She knew he worked at an office as some kind of financial trader. She knew he was good at it because they had more money than she had ever dreamed she would have.

But when he tried to explain stock market swings, algorithms, market capitalization and crypto currency, it was as if he was speaking a foreign language. When she cried because she didn't understand what he was saying, he told her not to worry, he would always take care of her.

And he had kept his word. She had a checking account in her name that always had plenty of money in it for anything she needed. And he refilled it every month without fail. Plus, she had many credit cards that were in her name, which Ron paid. Actually, Ron paid for everything.

And it's time to do some of that myself, April thought to herself. Cindy had been paying her a salary, but she had yet to cash the checks. When Cindy asked why, April said she just didn't feel like putting it into the bank account Ron had set up.

"Why not open another one on your own, then?" Cindy asked. April knew Cindy wanted to ask more about why she hadn't done it before, but she didn't.

Well, why haven't I? April asked herself. She knew the answer. It was another step to being more independent, and she was afraid that Ron wouldn't like it.

But then maybe he would be proud of me. If I told him. But April knew she wouldn't tell. Not because what she was about to do was wrong, but because she didn't want to do anything to make him unhappy or disturb the new life they were making together.

Checking her purse to make sure she had all the checks from work, she decided. Cindy's bank was just around the corner. She'd stop there, open an account, deposit the checks, and then head to the art gallery to spend Ron's money on the new house he insisted on getting.

As her head was down looking in her purse, April bumped into another woman walking the opposite way.

"Excuse me," April said. "I need to watch where I'm going."

"No worries," the woman replied, and hurried on.

April turned to look at the woman as she walked away and wondered if she had seen her before. She'd ask Cindy if there was a new woman in town. Something about it didn't feel right. If Cindy didn't know, she'd ask Judith.

But in the excitement of what she was doing with her new house, she forgot about the incident. It wasn't until later when Judith introduced them that she remembered the bump.

And it was not long after that she realized that the woman would change everything in her life.

Ten

After Mary picked up Rho and left with April, Bree shut the door and leaned up against it, smiling. It was so different from less than a year ago when she had dragged the box of mail into her house and then lay on the floor sobbing.

It had taken days for her to open the letter from Paul. She had been so angry at him for leaving. For having the audacity to get cancer and die. After reading his letter, she had realized that he had known about the cancer long before he told her.

He had spent months putting his plan together, researching what happened to her daughter, and hadn't told her. He made her find Mary on her own. It was such a wise plan. So like Paul, who knew her so well. Paul knew she would finally give in, and want to find her daughter.

And Paul understood that she would have to decide for herself to do it. She would have to let go of her pride and shame. Bree didn't know which was worse, the pride or the shame. Both had closed her off from life and her friends. And it had taken Paul's death, and his letter, and her friends forcing her to deal with it all, for her to fix what she had done and look for the daughter she had given up.

Remembering her past decisions always brought a wave of shame and guilt that sometimes still forced her to her knees. Today she remained standing, her back still against the door, and let herself remember what happened next.

After finally telling her friends about her daughter, and then thinking that she had lost her forever, she found her daughter where she least expected her to be—in Spring Falls.

Mary and her husband, Seth, had moved there a year before. They could have chosen anywhere to live. Why did they choose her home town? Paul must have had a hand in that decision, but what was it? There was no way to ask him.

Not that she hadn't tried. She talked to him silently in her head, and sometimes out loud, knowing she was fooling herself.

However, sometimes it felt as if he had never left, his presence so strong in the room that she would turn to him and then realize that his ashes were still in the box she had brought with her. A box she had buried in a drawer in her bedroom so she wouldn't see it.

Although Bree knew that someday she would have to do something with the ashes, she wasn't ready to face that decision yet. If she couldn't see the box, she could pretend sometimes that he was at work or running errands, and would be home soon.

Bree wondered if maybe her talking to him was why it felt as if he was still hanging around. Or she could be making it all up, letting her imagination run wild to keep the grief at bay.

After all, Bree reasoned, *I am a writer. I make stuff up.* Sometimes the stories she wrote were so real to her she'd forget they were stories. So she was making up a story that Paul was still around her.

But if he was there, she thought she knew why. There were things he hadn't told her, and maybe he wanted to. Maybe he wanted to tell her how Mary got to Spring Falls. But more likely, if he was still present, he was expecting her to do something she would not do. Ever.

She would not tell her secret. She knew Paul had never wanted her to keep what had happened a secret. He had asked her countless times if she was sure. And she had answered countless times that she was—finally getting so mad at him, that he gave up asking.

But Bree knew Paul well. He wouldn't just give up if he thought he was right. So even though the rational part of her knew he couldn't still be around—he was dead and gone forever—her heart kept telling her he was, and was still pushing her to speak. He was still imploring her to tell Mary who her father was. Who Rho's grandfather was.

Bree shook her head and stamped her foot. No, she wouldn't. She couldn't. It would break their hearts as it had broken hers. There was no way she was going to do it.

So just in case Paul was in the room, still not moving on his way into the light—if there was such a thing—she spoke to him out loud.

"No Paul, I am not telling. And I am fine now. If you are here, you can move on."

Then she laughed. How ridiculous was she, anyway? Did she think he was there? That he would tell her somehow that he was there?

But it made for a good story. Perhaps she could use it somehow. Now that her agent gave her the green light to go forward writing under her own name, she had some work to do. She had been making notes for months about what she would write, but still had some research and thinking to do first.

Although she never knew how a story would unfold before she wrote it, she knew how it would begin and end. That she didn't know yet. Bree knew people thought writing was only when you were typing words onto a page. But it was so much more than that.

The ideas, characters, thoughts, events, world building, were always going on in the background. Only after all that went on did the words flow for her. Now she was preparing something new, what it was, she wasn't sure.

The only thing she knew for sure was she had finished writing spicy romance under a pen name so no one would know her. It had been rewarding, and she loved writing them, but that was what she did when Paul was alive. And Bree knew that to fully live again, whatever she did when Paul was alive had to be finished so she could make a new life for herself.

Heading to the kitchen to make lunch before starting her afternoon of writing research, she could have sworn she heard Paul laugh. Once again, she told herself, her imagination was working overtime.

But as she made herself a salad, she thought about the woman named Grace who had known Paul when he was a teenager and how Grace had helped to unravel the mystery of where Paul had taken her baby daughter.

Didn't Grace mention she knew someone who could see people in the in-between? Bree asked herself.

If there was such a thing, perhaps Grace's friend could tell her if Paul was still around and get him to leave if he was.

Bree shook her head and laughed at herself again. There she was, caught up in her fantasies. Still, she hadn't properly thanked Grace for helping. Perhaps she could get Grace's number from Judith or Bruce and call to update her about what had happened since they last saw each other.

With that plan in mind, Bree took her salad out into the small garden behind the house, grabbing a book on her way out, and went out to do one of her favorite things. Read and eat at the same time, and in a garden. It pleased her to no end that reading was part of the job of being a writer.

Normally it would be much too cold to eat in the garden this time of year, but it had been unseasonably warm, and Bree wanted to take advantage of it. With a coat and hat on, it was perfect.

Bree sighed, feeling happier than she had felt since Paul had gotten sick. Her life was perfect, just the way it was. Finally. And even though the grief and shame would well up at the most inappropriate times, and she knew it would never go away, she could live with it now.

So once again, as she did at least once a day, she said, "Thank you, Paul," just in case he could hear her.

Eleven

April opened the door of Cindy's art gallery and stood, mouth open, staring at the scene in front of her.

Janet Parker was standing on her tiptoes at the top of a ladder while her wife Mimi Hart held it steady for her. Which at first glance seemed wrong. After all, Mimi was the tall one. Shouldn't she be at the top of the ladder instead of Janet? And what were they doing, anyway?

"What's going on here?" she yelped, afraid for Janet, who had a swag of twinkle lights hanging from one hand while holding on to the ladder with another.

Both of them glanced over their shoulders at April, Mimi clutching the ladder so hard her knuckles were white and making Janet sway a little off balance. which made April squeak in fear, imagining what could happen.

"We have it backward, don't we?" Janet said. "But I didn't realize how high these ceilings were until I climbed the ladder. And then Mimi came out and found me doing this by myself."

"Which was amazingly stupid," Mimi said, trying, and failing, not to scowl at Janet.

"Well, come down now!" April demanded, using the voice she had used when disciplining her children.

Laughing, Janet started down the ladder after saying, "Yes, mom!"

April beamed. Her fear for Janet dissipated as Janet's high-top sneakers touched the floor. She loved these two women. They had taught her so much about being free.

They were the ones who brought her back into the world when she first returned to Spring Falls, arranging for her sassy new hair cut and taking her shopping for new clothes. The short boots they bought that day were still her favorite.

And now they were teaching her all about Cindy's art business. Plus, seeing how they treated one another was showing her a different kind of love. One that didn't control, but supported. Like Mimi rushing to hold Janet's ladder, and proof reading Janet's writing. They were a team, and yet they were individuals. It was what she hoped her marriage with Ron would become.

"Really, what's going on, Mimi?" April asked, still using her mom voice.

Mimi didn't answer immediately, too busy hugging Janet to calm herself. Janet's short blond hair gelled into spikes tipped with multiple colors, just reached Mimi's chin. In contrast, Mimi's almost black hair was long and silky, often hanging down her back in a braid, or pulled into a ponytail. Today she had it piled on the top of her head, which looked both elegant and artsy at the same time.

"Holiday decorations!" Cindy said, coming into the gallery and answering April's question.

"But why are you doing it, Janet?"

"I saw the box of stuff and thought it would be fun?"

"No, and no!" Cindy said, laughing, looking up at the ceiling at what Janet had done so far.

Janet laughed too at her handiwork. It was a mess. Lights were hanging where they weren't supposed to be and the silver stars that she knew were supposed to hang down into the room were only a few feet from the wood beams that stretched from wall to wall.

When Cindy took over the building, she had the second floor removed above the gallery and the windows from the second floor poured light into the room. The art displayed in the gallery was constantly changing, and people loved stopping by to see what was new.

They knew they were welcome, even if they were not buying. Cindy wanted them to enjoy the space and art. She wanted her gallery to be a place that inspired and comforted. And if you wanted a piece of art, Cindy and her team were delighted to sell it to you.

Cindy was brilliant at both the design and marketing of her gallery, thinking of art not as something only people who comprised the art world would enjoy, but something everyone could understand and love. They often used the room as a community gathering space, hosted town meetings and even book clubs.

At the back of the gallery was the office where Cindy ran both the brick and mortar business and her thriving online sales. When Cindy discovered that both Janet and Mary wanted to be writers, she converted one of the small rooms in the back into a cozy space they called the writer's room.

There was still a second floor above those rooms, but it was rarely used, and April knew Cindy was thinking about opening up those upstairs rooms into a separate gallery space.

"I appreciate your enthusiasm, Janet," Cindy said, "but Seth is coming in to do this."

"Thank the gods," Janet said. "I just realized that isn't my skill. Besides, it's awesome that you are hiring Seth."

The Ruby Sisters, along with Janet and Mimi, had a mostly unspoken agreement to help Mary and her husband. Even before they learned Mary was Bree's daughter, they had all formed an attachment to her.

Now that she was truly part of the family, they were even more diligent. Seth worked for a construction company part time and as a handyman the rest of the time. All of them knew, through Mary, that his dream was to have his own construction company one day.

"He's fantastic at what he does. I've had him fix a few things at the house and he's done a great job. This should be a piece of cake for him, and I know they can use the money," Cindy said.

"Do you think he could help me with my new house?" April asked. "Ron hired someone already, but I could have Seth do things too, couldn't I?"

"Absolutely!" Cindy answered.

Just then the front door opened and a young couple walked in and Mimi stepped away to see if she could help them. But first, the couple looked up at the mess hanging off the beams and started laughing.

When Seth showed up a few moments later, he found them all standing in the center of the gallery, pointing at the ceiling and giggling. What Cindy hadn't noticed at first was that Janet had somehow hung the two angels upside down.

"What the?" he said, looking at the mess.

"Okay," Janet said. "I'm staying away from Christmas decorations on ceilings from now on."

"I'm on it," Seth said, giving Janet a hug.

"When you're done, Seth, can I talk to you about my new house?" April asked.

Seth's smile said it all. For Seth, a new baby, a loving wife, friends who supported them, and work that he wanted to do meant life was better than he had ever dreamed it could be.

They were all so busy laughing and planning that none of them noticed the woman standing across the street watching. Feeling envious. And wondering if she had a right to destroy all of that happiness. And what they would do to her when she did.

Twelve

April spent the next few hours in the gallery, helping Seth hang the holiday decorations. Not by standing on ladders—she was even shorter than Janet—but by pointing, suggesting, and collaborating, both of them enjoying working together.

By the time they were done, they had transformed the gallery with sparkling lights and tiny hanging mirrors. They chose not to hang the angels, thinking that it was too much.

"Maybe after Thanksgiving?" Janet asked, missing her upside down angels.

April shook her head. "Maybe never? Maybe a tree when we get closer to the holidays, but without the references that might make some people uncomfortable."

Seeing what April and Seth had done, Cindy agreed. It was perfect, just the way it was.

"Too bad you didn't video this as you did it," Janet said. "Mimi knows how to put it up on social media. It would help market the gallery, but also give people ideas about what they could do. And Seth could use it to help grow his business."

Cindy looked over at April and Seth and said, "You know, that's not a bad idea. Not the lights, of course, since they are already done. But why not video what you are going to do to your house, April? You have an excellent design eye, and I know Seth would be brilliant at carrying it out."

"It would help Seth build his business?" April asked, while thinking about how much fun it would be. It would be a way to help and do something she loved to do all at the same time.

"It would," Janet said. "Mimi and I could help you two set it up, but then Mary could help too. She's the one that keeps the writer's group together, so I know she has great organizational skills."

Seth and April looked at each other. April had a fleeting thought about how Ron would feel about her doing this business, especially with another man—even if he was young enough to be her son—and dismissed it.

Plus, Ron said she could do what she wanted with the house. And even though it was not the house she would have chosen for herself, she could make it into something that could open a new life for her, and help someone else at the same time. What could be better?

"Do you have anywhere you need to be right now, Seth?" She asked.

"I've got an hour."

"Shall we go look at my house and see what you think?"

Looking at Janet, he asked, "Will you really show us how to do the video stuff?"

"Can't wait," Janet said. "We'll figure it out together."

Seth grinned. "I'm all in."

"In what? And wow!" Mimi said, coming back into the gallery after answering the galleries' phone. "What have you done here? This is perfect! And what are you all in about, Seth?"

"Janet said you could show us how to make videos of what we do in April's house so I can use it to build my business."

Mimi sighed to herself, thinking it was one more thing on her plate, before saying, "Great idea! But not only that, it would help April to build a design business."

"'My own design business?" April said, barely getting the words out. How did Mimi know it was her dream? A whole new life doing something she loved to do?

She sunk down to the floor, back against the wall, and stuck her legs straight out in front of her and wondered how this had happened. Just last spring she had been alone in her house, kids grown and moved away, and Ron busy all day, sometimes not coming home for days. But always expecting her to be ready and waiting for him when he got home. And that had been her life. Until the day Judith gave her the courage to come home to Spring Falls. And now her friends were giving her the courage to have a life of her own, doing something she had always loved, designing things.

On the floor looking up at the lights, and Seth, Cindy, Janet, and Mimi smiling down at her, she began to cry. Not huge sobs, just a small whimper of happiness at what could happen if she wanted it to. Mittens, the gallery cat, seeing an opportunity, made his way over to her lap and sat down, purring away.

Cindy sat down beside her and then, leaning in, said, "April, you are allowed to do this. All of us will help. Wait until the rest of the Ruby Sisters hear about this idea. They'll all be pitching in."

April looked down into Mitten's yellow-green eyes, and then into Cindy's brown ones, feeling a wave of delight roll in through her entire body, and said, "Okay, I'm all in, too. Now help me get off the dang floor."

A few minutes later, Seth and April had driven off in Seth's battered red truck, and Mimi and Janet were busy with customers who, attracted by the sparkling lights, had come in to see the space and the art. Cindy returned to her office, alone.

She sighed. Now that all the excitement was over, she needed to get back to work. But she couldn't stop thinking about April and her decision to work with Seth. April had changed since coming back to Spring Falls. Well, not changed so much as become herself again. And that made Cindy a little worried for her friend. What would Ron think of all this?

And since she tried to be truthful, even to herself, she had to admit that she also felt a little sad, knowing that April might not be at the gallery as much as she had been before, and even Mimi and Janet were excited about the idea. Did that mean she would lose all of them if the idea was successful?

Stop it, she said to herself. *You want them to be happy.* And she knew that was true, but Cindy knew that it was also true that she felt a little jealous. Maybe she needed a makeover, too.

What I need is a mental makeover, Cindy mumbled to herself. *And so does Marsha.*

Because Cindy knew that one thing that made her feel better was to be of service, she decided she would come up with something for Marsha to do. Cindy knew she needed something to take her mind off of her lack of her artistic skills. It might as well be something that helped a friend.

Cindy sank down in the office chair she had bought when she first opened the gallery and tried to feel good about herself. But she was truly discouraged and couldn't bring herself to tell anyone. Everyone thought she was happy working on her paintings. But she knew the truth.

None of what she was painting was any good. She might own a gallery, but she wasn't an artist. It didn't matter that people once thought she was, or even that she once thought she was. They were all wrong. She wasn't. She just couldn't find the spark that used to be there.

Sighing, she turned back to the business at hand, and said a prayer of gratitude for the chance to have a business and friends she loved. They were all safe and secure. What more could she want for herself, or anyone else?

Thirteen

It didn't take Ron long to find out what was happening in Spring Falls having installed spyware on April's phone years before. Alone in the house in Silver Lake, he threw the pen he was holding against the wall, where it flew apart, flinging parts everywhere.

At least I didn't throw the phone, Ron thought as he picked up the parts. There it was again, that temper he thought he had conquered long ago. That same temper that had gotten him into the predicament that resulted in him and April living apart most of the time.

And it left him conflicted. He liked what was happening for himself. Having the house all to himself gave him all the freedom that he craved. But he hated it because he had no control over what April was doing when he wasn't around. Now she was starting a design business with that Seth guy? How could this be happening?

I need to control this, Ron muttered to himself.

And then, as he often did when alone, he had a conversation with himself.

But if you control it with your temper, all of your life could fall apart.

Well then, how do you expect me to stop her?

Perhaps you don't.

Why not?

Are you happy here alone in this house, Ron?

Ron paused before he answered himself.

Yes.

Are you able to do what you want with no one noticing?

Yes.

So you are actually better off than you were before?

Maybe.

Well, let's count the ways. You have a business that makes so much money you can't spend it all. You have a wife who loves you and doesn't bug you about what you do with your time. She is now happy with what you have given her, so she will be even less interested in your business. And when you do see her, she is everything you ever wanted in a wife.

During this conversation with himself, Ron had been pacing back and forth in his home office. The sun was filtering through the half-open blinds, sparkling off the dust motes in the air, reminding him that April wasn't there to clean the house anymore. For a moment, he felt like kicking the wall.

But playing back the conversation he had just had with himself, he realized he was better off now. He could hire a cleaning person, spend a little money to have a clean house. How easy was that?

Of course, he had to make sure he locked up private business stuff when he wasn't home, not leaving it out as he had become used to since April didn't live there anymore. He'd install a few cameras just in case.

I should have done that long ago, he thought.

Maybe, maybe not, the voice in his head said. Remember, you don't want people to ever see what you have been doing, either.

And now, perhaps a husbandly phone call to your wife?

Hum. Yes, let's see if she lies to me by not saying anything about her new adventure.

Picking up his phone, Ron walked out into the hall to make the phone call. He did it out of habit. Always be sure no one is listening.

Standing in front of the hallway mirror as he waited for April to pick up, Ron again saw the man he had become and smiled at himself. He looked exactly like what he wanted to look. Wealthy, just good looking enough to be approachable, and very, very trustworthy.

April had been expecting Ron's call. Not because she knew Ron had found out about her new business idea, but because she knew Ron was a good husband. Now that they were apart more often, he was checking in more than he used to, and she loved it.

But she was struggling with how much she would tell him. It wasn't until she moved back to Spring Falls that she fully realized how much she had lived alone all those years in Silver Lake. She kept the children's acting up out of his life and smoothed everything down for him. She had felt he worked so hard she had to make sure his home life was peaceful and perfect.

But now April wondered if that was why she had done that. Maybe she hadn't told him things because she was afraid of what he would say.

Where did this fear come from? April asked herself. She used to be so carefree and lighthearted. Her friends called her a chipmunk, full of energy. And her parents called her their little wren. Where had that chipmunk and wren gone for all those years?

It doesn't matter, April decided. Chipmunk and Wren were back, or at least returning. Which meant she had to—no, wanted to—tell Ron everything she was doing. She would expect him to be happy for her.

She was going to have a business of her own. He would be proud of her.

April thought back to that afternoon and what she and Seth had discussed. They decided that for now other builders would do the big stuff since Seth didn't have the equipment to do it all himself. But she and Seth would decide together what to do with each room.

What Seth could do himself, he would, while acting as the foreman for the project. They had only talked for the hour, but that had been long enough for them both to realize what a good idea Janet had given them.

So when Ron called, April was ready to tell him everything, and when she felt his smile, she bubbled over with excitement.

For his part, Ron did his best. He kept his smile. He kept his calm. *Even after all she has told me,* Ron thought. *there is no reason to be upset.* She wasn't the one keeping secrets. All she wanted from him was some enthusiasm for her new idea.

He had already promised her all the money she would need to create her dream house and garden. He hadn't realized how much she would need, and he knew she didn't either, having not done it before, but he had plenty of money to give her.

It made him proud that he had what she needed, and that she wanted him to be part of the project.

He didn't want to be, but he liked that she wanted to include him. So he kept his smile going during the entire conversation. He meant it when he told her he loved her, and he felt the impact of her love for him, so there was no reason to be unhappy.

That's what he told himself. But he knew it wasn't true. He was unhappy. And frustrated. It was time to plan a little trip to take care of those feelings.

Fourteen

After her coffee with Cindy, Judith had gone into her office expecting it to be a normal day. Her job, as she saw it, was to make sure everything in town ran smoothly.

Everything running smoothly wasn't really a stretch, in her opinion. She really wanted everything to run smoothly, and she believed she could do it. She had the power to make it so because she knew almost everyone in town and their business.

The problem was that even though her business was taking care of other businesses, businesses were made up of people, not just numbers. Which meant that even though Judith knew she shouldn't, she often felt responsible for people's individual lives running smoothly, too.

But Judith knew that kind of responsibility would eventually make her crazy, so she tried to limit herself to being in charge of only the people that she worked with, and only when they were on the clock.

To make sure her business ran smoothly, the first thing Judith did every morning was make sure everyone knew what they had to do that day. Her thought was if she taught her people well, they would take care of their people, and that care would roll out into the community, making everything run smoothly.

If only it were that easy, she said to herself as she checked her hair and makeup in the mirror before logging into the Zoom call. She might want everything to run smoothly, but Judith was also a pragmatist. She knew that it usually didn't.

They used Zoom for meetings because all the people working for her, except her assistant, Nancy, were independent bookkeepers and accountants, and they were rarely in the office. They'd stop by to show her things she needed to know, or hold their client meetings in the conference room, but mostly, it was just her and Nancy in the office.

So this morning, like every Monday morning after coffee with Cindy, Judith ran a Zoom meeting to prepare everyone for the week. She expected every person on her team to be on the call. Even if they were on vacation.

Once they learned she was serious about that requirement, they were always there. The only time someone missed that meeting was if there was a family emergency. And they had all learned that in spite of, or maybe because of, her need to make things right, Judith was always supportive when their excuse involved family.

Although Judith requested that no one ever share what she did, they all knew that many of them had been the recipients of Judith's generosity in times of trouble. They knew they could count on Judith to provide support, sometimes funds, and would always work behind the scenes to get to the heart of the problem and be part of the solution.

So, although there was a bit of fear in their hearts about Judith and her fiery determination to make things right, they loved her for it. And she knew it. And she treasured that, because she loved them, too.

As long as they stayed within the guidelines of doing the right thing at all times, to the best of their ability. Well, even then she might still love them, but their time of working with her would be over if they intentionally did wrong.

Today she had a hard time keeping her mind on what she was doing during the meeting. There were things going on that made little sense to her. Only years of managing her business kept her on track during the call, and she thought no one had noticed how distracted she was.

Ninety minutes later, every client they were working with had been discussed. Even though they each worked with different people, their clients' businesses often overlapped. Sharing information made them a powerful and effective group of people. And if anyone ever breathed a word of what they learned in one of these meetings to anyone outside the meeting, they knew Judith would fire them.

There were no second chances if they leaked information. And if that information hurt someone, Judith would be like a fiery angel of vengeance, and have them prosecuted to the highest letter of the law.

For Judith, loyalty was everything. Loyalty and truth-telling. It was something she tried to live up to herself, so she was feeling guilty about not telling everyone about meeting with Bruce. She was keeping secrets from her friends. Not secrets that needed to remain secrets. It was about her. She was afraid of what was happening with Bruce. And she knew he was too.

But her continuing relationship with Bruce, even after the mystery of Paul's last gift to Bree was solved, was something her friends should know about. Didn't they all agree not to keep secrets from each other anymore? Judith resolved to tell them at their next dinner together, which was only a few days away. It was going to be at her house this time, which would make it easier, since she was most comfortable in her own place.

But it wasn't just her relationship with Bruce that was distracting her. It was the stranger in town. The one she kept seeing out of the corner of her eye. The one who tried to disappear, but that only made her stand out to Judith. No one knew who she was. However, it wasn't just that the woman was a stranger acting strange, there was something else going on.

Perhaps it's just my suspicious nature, Judith said to herself. But she didn't believe it was just that. Her spidey senses were tingling. Something was happening that needed to be addressed. It was time for her to find out who the woman was.

But since she didn't know a single thing about her to do any kind of research, she decided there was only one thing to do.

Track her down and get answers.

Fifteen

The woman invading Judith's thoughts was sitting in her room, chewing her thumbnail. It was a bad habit she tried to break, but in times like this, she couldn't stop.

Bumping into that woman had been a bad idea. All of it was a bad idea. Coming to Spring Falls. Watching those women. *All stupid ideas, just like you,* Nicky said to herself.

But the problem with herself had started long before she arrived in Spring Falls. And when Sara disappeared, bad ideas became her world. Before then, Nicky considered herself a normal girl, if a little too private, and a little wild, living in a small normal town having a normal life with normal parents.

Whatever normal means, Nicky thought. *Was anyone normal?*

Nicky knew that whatever normal was, she wasn't anymore, probably never had been. But she had gotten away with it until Sara went missing. And then everything that held her together fell apart.

It happened so quickly, out of nowhere. A normal life transformed overnight. The family had breakfast together as they normally did. Or so she heard. Since she had moved away. But that's what her mom and dad told her, and the police, and anyone else who she would talk to.

"Yes," her mom would say repeatedly, trying to rewrite history. "Yes, Sara had her normal breakfast of that stupid sugary cereal that she liked. Yes, she was excited about school. She was trying out for cheerleading later that day. No, she never made it to the tryouts."

During the inquiry about Sara's disappearance, the family learned Sara didn't need to tryout. Everyone had already agreed Sara had to be on the squad. In a town as small as theirs, they knew who could do what.

Nicky knew that Sara would have been overjoyed. She could see Sara in her mind's eye, jumping with joy, her blond hair loose from her ponytail. Laughing and hugging her friends. But that never happened. Sara was gone, and no one knew where she had gone to.

When Nicky learned Sara had disappeared, she returned home to help. But by then, her mother was hysterical, and her father was numb. After that, they got angry with her, as if it was her fault. If she would have stayed home, it never would have happened.

Nicky was not allowed to say Sara's name. She could not ask about her. There was very little to say and much to avoid. The police came and went, and after a few weeks, when there were no answers, everyone shut down.

Her father had been a responsible man, and a loving father, but that was before. Afterwards, he lost all the qualities he used to have. He just sat in a room doing nothing, silently crying. He would not talk to his wife or Nicky. He would not even talk to himself.

Over time, Nicky's skills had slowly dissolved until she felt as if she was completely useless. The life Nicky might have lived disappeared with Sara.

Instead, she never married, never had good friends, moved from place to place, first trying to forget and then looking for her sister.

For years Nicky wouldn't admit to herself that was what she was doing, but once she admitted that to herself she had searched with a vengeance.

Yes, Nicky thought, *vengeance was a good word to use.* She knew the *Bible* said that God said, "Vengeance is mine." But didn't he need someone to carry out that act for Him? After all these years of moving from town to town looking for Sara, she had discovered that thousands and thousands of women go missing every year. Sometimes they are found, usually they are not.

Her sister was just one of those numbers, and she had so little to go on. The one thing she had always known for sure was that her sister would never have run away. She had everything going for her.

Yes, Sara would have left town someday. She wanted to see the world. But she hadn't been in a hurry. Nicky knew Sara had been one of those rarities—a happy teenager.

But now, after all these years, Nicky thought she knew what had happened and who had done it. But she couldn't prove it by herself. She needed someone who would believe her, and fight to right what was wrong.

Everything in her gut told her that the person was Judith Zoe. But would she help her? Why would she? She didn't know Sara. Still, she was going to make the plea of her life to her and pray that what she had heard about her was true: that Judith Zoe fought for what was right.

Nicky wondered if she should change into something more appropriate to meet with the woman, something that fit going into a successful business woman's office, but decided against it. She knew Judith had seen her. If she changed her appearance now, it might seem deceptive. And that was the last thing she could afford to be.

Twenty minutes later Nicky opened the door of Judith's office, and found her standing there, purse slung over her shoulder.

They stared at each other. Nicky tilting her head up to look straight into Judith's blue eyes until Judith said, "I was just heading out to find you."

Nicky didn't answer, understanding how a deer in headlights must feel. Judith pointed at her office door and said, "Let's talk in there."

Nicky knew there was no turning back now. This was her chance. Could she explain what she knew clearly enough to get the help she needed? What she had to tell her would affect Judith and her friends. If it was true. And Nicky was pretty sure that it was.

Judith's office was like Judith. Straight-forward and unexpectedly comfortable. Only a few pictures hung on the wall. Her office chair looked firm and sturdy with a leather seat, and a metal back.

Judith sat down and rested her hands on the desk. Her short nails hinted at someone who didn't have time for things that weren't necessary. The desk was free of papers. and a credenza held a beautiful flower arrangement.

Behind Judith, the light from a window highlighted her hair, but made it hard to see her, which Nicky realized was the point. She was the one in the spotlight. It was as if she were an actress just learning her lines. She could tell the truth or make something up.

Judith paused, staring at the woman sitting in front of her, before saying, "Let's hear it. Hold nothing back."

At that moment, something broke open in Nicky's heart. Nicky felt a rush of gratitude, a gratitude that made her feel numb and empty at the same time, because what she had been waiting for all this time had finally happened. Here was someone who would listen. Finally. And she was ready to talk. Finally.

But she was the only one who truly knew what disaster she was bringing, and for the first time, felt sorry about it. Still, it had to be done.

Sixteen

It was hunger that woke Marsha up. Well, not exactly woke her up. Made her get up. Marsha didn't even bother to glance at the clock. She barely remembered Cindy leaving to go to the gallery. She only knew that Cindy had left hours ago.

She had meant to get up. Instead, she had simply groaned and pulled the sheets over her head and disappeared into sleep again. The snuggly comforter that Cindy had put on her bed for the winter and the heated mattress pad made the bed warm, cozy, and safe. Marsha felt like a bear in a cave hiding from the world.

Not that Marsha didn't know what she was doing. She recognized depression when she saw it. After all, she had lived with this problem for years. She knew her mood swings well. Except they weren't the kind of mood swings from crazy happy to deeply sad. She knew she wasn't bi-polar. Years ago in New York, she had herself tested just in case.

No, her mood swings were from kinda happy to very sad. She thought she had dealt with her mood swings long ago, but since she had come to Spring Falls, she had lost control of them.

Funny, she said to herself. *As if I don't know why.*

But that was the problem, really. She didn't want to remember why. Besides, truthfully, there was more than one reason, and there was nothing she could do about any of them.

Marsha recognized that to get out of her depression, she had to do something right now that pleased her. Not something to fix the past. Not something to plan for her future—whatever that was going to be. Something to do right now.

Well, you could eat, she said to herself. *And go outside. Take a walk. Or clean up Cindy's garden for her, getting it ready for the winter. Or find a place to live by yourself and let Cindy have her house back.*

Lying in bed staring at the ceiling, Marsha contemplated all those scenarios. And thought of some more. *Volunteer to babysit Mary's new baby. Help April with her new house. Get in shape. Find a dance class and take it. Or yoga.*

"Do something," her inner voice kept nudging her. "Do anything. Help yourself by helping someone else. No matter how small. It will work. I promise."

But what if I don't want it to work? Marsha asked that little voice. *What if I like it just the way it is?*

"You don't," it said.

"I do like it this way, and I don't care!" Marsha answered, silencing the voice for the time being.

But she and the voice knew she was lying. She cared. She was just afraid to hope for something good to happen to her. And she recognized that as the whiny part of herself. Many, many good things had happened for her, including the Ruby Sisters, who were giving her time to get over herself.

She could feel herself not wanting to be grateful, wanting to stay depressed because it was easier. Recognizing that was a dangerous place to be, Marsha rolled her eyes at herself and decided it really was time to do something.

Sighing, Marsha threw the covers off her, turned off the mattress pad, swung her legs off the bed with a groan, and got up, telling herself that it was not because of anything the voice said, but because she was hungry and had to pee.

Once in the bathroom, she decided to take a shower, and it was in the shower that Marsha finally broke down and cried for all that she had told no one, for all the things that had made her sad, and because she didn't know what to do with herself now.

Feeling marginally better, she made April's favorite peanut butter sandwich with banana chips in it for herself, thinking that if April liked it, it might work some kind of magic on her because now April was making a new life for herself. Just as she was washing the last of it down with her diet soda, her mobile pinged.

Well, maybe it is magic, she thought, because it was Bree asking if she wanted to take a walk in the woods with her. Mary had collected Rho, and she was at loose ends.

Marsha put her plate in the dishwasher, cleaning up after herself while she thought about it. She could say no, but then what would she do for the rest of the day? Or she could say yes and go outside with Bree.

Recognizing that if she went with Bree she was deciding to get on with her life, she texted back, "yes."

"Pick you up in fifteen minutes," was the response. Which didn't leave her much time to get ready for a walk in the woods. Which was probably Bree's way of making sure she didn't change her mind.

"I forgot how beautiful the woods are at this time of year," Marsha said.

The two of them were sitting on a bench along the trail that led to the tiny falls that the town was named for. The trail had always been there, but not the bench. Or if it had, they hadn't needed it when they were young and could run the trail, laughing the entire way.

Today, they needed a bench. And that was part of what made Marsha sad. She wasn't young anymore. None of them were. What could she possibly do with the rest of her life that made a difference?

The woods were transitioning between fall and winter. Some leaves remained, but mostly they carpeted the forest floor like a multicolored rug, their musky-sweet smell embracing the women, bringing back memories of shuffling through leaves on the way to school. Between the bare tree branches, the sky was bright blue, and the sun filtered through with long yellow streaks of light.

Bree sighed and said, "It is beautiful, isn't it? This transition. I used to think it was sad the trees lost their leaves, and then I realized it's probably a joy. The trees get to let go, and rest, and rebuild again with deeper roots, so they can expand more into the world in their next season.

"Trees are wonderful creatures. As they grow, and even in what looks like death, they are nurturing themselves and everything and everyone around them."

Marsha said nothing at first. She knew Bree well enough to know she was using the trees as a metaphor. Not just for herself, but for her, too.

"I see what you are saying, but I don't know what I am transitioning to. The tree knows itself as a tree. I don't know myself right now if I am not a dancer and teacher."

Bree turned to look at Marsha. "I think you might be missing the point. You are who you are, now and forever. The only difference between us and the tree is we get to choose what kind of branches to grow and fruit to produce.

"I am a writer. That's the trunk of my tree. I use words to express myself and share. What I do with that now may differ from what I did when Paul was alive. Nevertheless, that's me. You are a dancer and a teacher. What you do with that now could be different from what you did before. But I see you as that tree. Do you?"

"But you danced too. And you don't call yourself a dancer."

"Now see, Marsha, that's the glory of being this thing we call human. We can do and be almost anything. But what do I do that makes me feel most like myself? I write. Everything else I do supports that, including still dancing in my room when no one is looking. What do you do that makes you feel like yourself?"

"This sounds like the talk you gave me when we were going to college. You said I knew what I wanted to do and be."

"And you did, didn't you?"

"So I have to like transitions?"

"Well, it makes life a lot easier," Bree laughed. "And trust me, I know!"

Seventeen

After talking to Ron, April spun around, arms outstretched, in what she thought would become the living room, and said out loud to the walls, "This was the best day ever!"

Now the room didn't feel empty. It felt ready to be transformed. As the last light of the day shone through the dirty windows and revealed a stained, but potentially beautiful wood floor, she added, "This is all so perfect. This is my future!"

She didn't care that anyone passing by might see her. Although the possibility of that happening was remote since an enormous maple tree blocked the view from the street. Still, she didn't care. In fact, she would have welcomed it. She envisioned the day when her house would be filled with people.

It would be so different from her home in Silver Lake, where no one came to visit and days would often go by with no one to talk to but Ron when he was home. And the kids when they were young. As they got older and developed lives of their own, their conversations comprised only a few short sentences, if she was lucky. For a moment, April wondered once again how it had come to that, how she had become so isolated?

April shook off the past, breathed in the sweet and musty air of a house that needed her, and smiled.

Who would have thought the day would turn out so well? That morning, staring at the house with Ron by her side, excited about what he was showing her, she had felt doomed. Trapped into living in a house she didn't want. It was too big. It felt like a monster that was going to eat up her days. Not cozy. Not beautiful. In desperate need of repairs.

That morning, she had wondered why Ron bought her a house that needed so much work. Probably because it was the biggest house close to town. It meant he could show off and give her what she asked for at the same time. What the house looked like then didn't matter to him. Money could fix it.

Maybe I am misunderstanding him, April thought. Perhaps he knew she would enjoy fixing it. If so, he had given her the best gift she could ever have received.

However, that morning, she had simply accepted this was the house, quietly thanked him, trying to hide the fact that she felt slightly hysterical. All she could think about then was the work involved in making the house liveable, and embarrassed about the enormity of it.

Going to see Bree and taking care of baby Rho had helped her get over her upset about what—at the time—felt like a burden. Bree was so happy about the new direction of her writing and about having her daughter and granddaughter in her life, that it reminded April that Paul's last gift to Bree had been a gift to all of them.

And Rho was the sweetest baby ever, totally adored by every member of the Ruby Sisters. Mary and Seth had made them all Rho's godmothers, and they all would have to do their best not so spoil her too much.

Afterward, while walking to the gallery, a kernel of excitement about the house had grown. By the time she reached the gallery, she was ready to share her new idea. Seth's coming to the rescue and fixing Janet's poorly hung decorations had further fueled that idea. She could hire Seth to help her. But it was Janet's brilliant idea about videoing what she did with her house, and sharing it on social media, that made it into the best day ever.

She could support Seth's business, and help Mary and Rho by doing something she loved to do. And maybe, just maybe, she could build a small business for herself too.

"I can do this!" April yelled, and laughed in delight at the echo of her words bouncing off the cathedral ceiling back to her.

While waiting for Judith to pick her up, she walked around the house with the notebook and erasable pen that Mimi had given her before she left the gallery, saying she would need it. That and a tape measure. How right Mimi had been.

When she and Seth walked from room to room together, she had scribbled down ideas as Seth measured walls and windows. It was only the beginning. She would need many more hours to figure out what she wanted to do, but that made it even more exciting.

April envisioned a life full of possibilities, both for her and her house. She felt as if a thousand ideas were hitting her at once. Each idea was like a bee flitting from flower to flower, pollinating the next. She could barely keep up with them.

In the back of her mind, April wondered if she was being a little excessive. But she told herself she had a right to do this, to spend Ron's money. He said she could, and now she wanted to.

After all, for all these years, she had followed the rules of life with Ron. Of course, she loved him, and she knew he loved her, and that was why she had gone along with it all. Besides, they were raising children, and that left little time to do things for herself. And when she married, she had promised herself that she wouldn't be so much like her parents, always flitting around from idea to idea.

But now it was different. Now she was home again, and she was transforming herself along with the house. Not into someone new as much as back to who she was inside, but with all the wisdom she had gained through the years. And nothing could stop her now. She had Ron, she had money, and she had friends, ideas, and the freedom to express them.

For a moment she felt a shiver of cold, and a flicker of fear passed through her. But she ignored it. Of course she was cold. It was cold outside. Besides, the house was old and drafty and the furnace probably needed to be replaced. There was nothing to worry about. She and the house would transform each other.

What April didn't know was how much of her entire life would be transformed. She'd live through it, but barely.

Eighteen

As Nicky poured out her story, Judith leaned back in her chair and listened, only asking enough questions to keep Nicky talking. From time to time, Nicky would pause and take tiny sips of water.

Then, making sure that Judith was still listening, launch back into the story, giving time for Judith to study Nicky to see past the exterior blandness that she had been projecting.

Yes, on the surface, Nicky had accomplished what she had wanted to accomplish—to disappear, be nobody, and have no one to care about or to care for her. It was glaringly obvious that losing her sister haunted Nicky. Made her act like a ghost. But as she talked, Judith caught a glimmer of the true Nicky shining through despite her best efforts to hide it.

In the middle of the story about her missing sister, Judith raised her hand to stop her talking. She stepped out into her office and asked her assistant, Nancy, to cancel all her appointments for the day, and to give Cindy a call and ask her if she would come to the office, right now, please.

"Is everything okay?" Nancy asked.

She had a glimpse of the woman in Judith's office when the door opened, and it was not anyone she had ever seen before. She shivered for a moment in response. There was definitely something off about that woman

"Yep. Tell Cindy not to worry. I just need a little help with something."

Seeing Nancy's concern, she smiled, "It's really okay. I just need another set of eyes and ears."

Pointing at the door, Nancy asked, "Can I get her anything?"

"Probably. But let's wait a beat first."

Nancy nodded, and picked up her phone as Judith slipped back into her office, shutting the door quietly behind her.

During the brief moments Judith had been gone, Nicky had slumped deeper into her chair, and had to straighten herself to talk again.

"Don't worry, I just asked my assistant to get us something. Now, before we go back to the story about you and your sister, I need to ask you a few simple questions."

"Okay?" Nicky said, shuddering a little, worried about what Judith would ask.

"What is the actual color of your hair?"

"Excuse me?"

"Your actual hair color, and what color are your eyes? I want to see the real Nicky. What do you really look like?"

Nicky stared at Judith, thinking it might be time to leave. She had been on her own most of her life. Maybe she should keep it that way. But the thought of her sister, perhaps alone somewhere, gave her a jolt of courage. She had come this far. She had to continue.

Reluctantly, Nicky unzipped a pocket in her jacket and pulled out a picture encased in plastic, and handed it to Judith.

"When?"

"Right before Sara disappeared. She was fifteen, and I was twenty."

Judith felt emotion flooding through her, causing her face to flush, and she knew that was a sign that she was about to get involved with something that would disrupt everything. She wished it wasn't happening. She had other things to do. But this was who she was.

Her friends teased her about her drive to right what was wrong, all of them knowing she couldn't help herself. If she saw wrong—and she could do something about it—she had to. And whatever had happened to Nicky's sister was wrong.

She stared at the two girls in the picture, and let herself feel what they felt for each other. The petite blond girl with striking blue eyes, was being hugged by her slightly taller, thinner sister, with darker hair but the same striking blue eyes. She made her decision. She had to help.

Through the fake hair color and contact lenses, Judith could see Nicky as that young woman—the woman she used to be before this horror came into her life. Nicky was still thin, but no longer wiry thin, scrawny thin. like a cat gone feral with no one looking out for it. Now that cat had come to her door. She couldn't turn it away.

Fear of what was coming made the hair on the back of Judith's neck stand up. She could almost feel the fear making its way from the soles of her feet to the tip of her hair. In her mind's eye, her red hair flashed for a second, and faded again.

Sighing, she closed her eyes, and then sat up straighter and asked the obvious question.

"Why come to Spring Falls? Do you think Sara is still alive? And that she is here?"

Nicky shook her head. "No. She's not here. I don't know if she is still alive. I doubt it. But I have to hope that she is until the day it's proved to me she has died. No. I am here because I think that the person who did something to her has lived here."

"Lived here? Or is still here?"

"Both?" Nicky asked, wishing Judith would stop asking questions. The courage she had worked up to bring herself to Judith had faded. Nicky closed her eyes, and in that moment felt herself slip away.

"I'm so tired," she whispered, and slumped to the floor.

Nineteen

R on poured himself a drink. It wasn't something he normally allowed himself to do. He always thought it was incredibly stupid that on TV shows, people came home from work and headed straight to their stash of liquor.

Since he and April had always commented on how no one did things like that, she would have wondered why he was drinking now. Not that she was a prude about drinking. It was that she had made a decision about not drinking for herself and expected Ron to be her partner in that decision.

Although April's parents hadn't been drinkers, Ron knew that Marsha and Bree had mothers who drank too much and made their daughters' lives miserable. Eventually, both of them died because of it. And that had sealed the deal for April. She would not be that kind of mother.

But now she didn't live there anymore, and he was alone. So on the way home, he stopped at a liquor store and bought himself a bottle of bourbon, the best they had. As he swirled the amber liquid in his glass, he thought about his father.

That piece of work, he said to himself.

Drunk and abusive would not even begin to describe his father. It was too mild a description. Besides, his father had no class. He would never drink bourbon. Just beer, the cheapest he could find.

Empty red and gold cans of Schmidt's beer were everywhere, crunching under his father's feet as he stomped through the house, looking for someone to abuse. Not someone. His son.

For some reason, his father hated him. Ron had often wondered if he was not really that man's son, and that's why he hated him. Or perhaps he wanted that to be true because he didn't want to be the son of a man like that.

He had built his entire life around not being like that man. And now, here he was, drinking. But not like his father. He was not a drunk. Or abusive. Or loud. Or low class.

Ron had learned early how the sounds of the beer cans crunching would change when his father was serious about finding him. By the time he was six, Ron had learned how to escape ahead of the tyrant looking for him and hide in the woods behind the house.

He wouldn't have been hard to find if his father had bothered to come to look for him. But first his father would have to negotiate the piles of junk that lay in the yard. But he rarely did. It would have been too much work.

Instead, his father would grab more drink and pass out. Never in the same place. Just where the last beer would finally take him down for the night.

His mother would stand silently by letting it all happen. Sometimes sitting in a chair, sometimes in the kitchen drinking her own can of beer, sometimes watching, most often turned away—not looking, obviously not caring.

Ron didn't understand why his father had never touched his mother. Just him. Maybe his father was afraid of his mother. He knew he was. She wasn't kind or thoughtful.

She just did what was expected. Sent him off to school, in almost clean clothes, giving him just enough change to buy some food since there wasn't much in the house.

There were no hugs or kisses, none of the things that April had lavished on their children, and even on him. That's one of many reasons he cherished April. She was the exact opposite of his mother.

For years Ron had searched his memory for a time his mother stood up for him, tried to protect him, and he couldn't find it. Eventually, his silent mother had run away, and left him there to deal with his father on his own. And he had. He learned that if he found friends, he could go to their house for a night, or days at a time.

He hid what was happening at home, so he could stay in school. He watched his friend's mothers and how they washed clothes, made food, and learned how to do it for himself. Sometimes they did it for him.

Looking back, Ron realized that his friends' mothers suspected what was happening at home, and did what they could to help him, but never speaking out. Strangely, he was glad about that. He kept his secret and so did they. He learned how to pretend. And he dreamed of the day he would be somebody.

How his father kept a job was a mystery to him. Somehow, his father showed up at work and did enough to not get fired. It probably helped that he worked away from home. He never really understood what his father did for the company he worked for. He didn't want to know.

Sometimes his father would have to travel. He loved it when his father was gone. Peace would reign for a few days. As he got older, his father would make him go with him. Probably to keep his son out of trouble while he was gone.

Ron hated those trips. His father's smell filling the cabin of the beat up truck. Cigarettes and booze stink puffing out of the ripped seats when he sat down. Rolling the windows down only made it worse. Dust, manure, noise added to the overwhelming anger that would sometimes roar through him. He learned to control it. Not wanting to be like his father. A raging bull.

And look at him now. He had done it. He was the exact opposite of his father. Successful beyond his father's wildest dreams, if he had any. Careful, meticulous, calm, and methodical. And April was his strength. Since the moment he met her, he had claimed her as his rock.

He leaned back in his chair thinking about how much he missed her, happy that she had found something to do with the house he had bought her, and silently happy that the house was so quiet, and all his.

Once again, thinking that perhaps this next phase of their life together wouldn't be so bad after all. Now he had the freedom he needed and a wife who pleased him and gave him strength.

Staring into his glass, Ron realized he was happy. Especially since everything was in place for his next trip.

Twenty

"What are we going to do with her?" Cindy asked Judith and Nancy. "Do you think there is something wrong with her? Should we take her to a doctor? Who is she anyway?"

The three women were huddled together in the waiting room of Judith's office, while Nicky lay on the couch shivering in the office.

As soon as Cindy got Nancy's phone call, she had rushed down the street to Judith's, worried despite what Nancy had said, and arrived just in time to hear Judith call out, "Water!"

Heart pumping, she had flung herself through the door to find Judith holding some strange woman up and trying to get her to drink water from the glass in her hand. Placing her hand on her heart, Cindy forced herself to breathe in and out slowly. Judith was okay.

Everything is okay, she kept saying to herself.

It was only after Judith had placed the woman on the couch and ushered them both out into the waiting room that Cindy's heart calmed down enough for her to pay attention to what was happening.

"I don't know what we are going to do with her. I don't know what's wrong with her, but I don't think it's something that requires a doctor. She just fainted." Judith said.

Nancy and Cindy waited for her to go on, but Judith hesitated before speaking.

"Look, she just told me the strangest story. I don't know why she came to me. But I do know that now that she did, I have to help.

"Nancy, could you find out from her where she has been staying, have her call ahead and give the okay for you to get her stuff? I want to move her to my house."

Nancy nodded, and a few minutes later, she left by the back door, saying she'd be back in a few minutes.

"You are seriously going to bring that stranger into your house? You know there is something off about her, don't you? And you still haven't told me who she is."

"Yes, I am. She's new in town, and looking for help, and I think, with what she told me, the Ruby Sisters are going to need to get involved. Whether or not we like it. So it's best to have her where we know where she is and can keep an eye on her. Besides, she needs friends. Being a friend is something we all know how to do. If it turns out we can't help, at least we can get her back on her feet."

"I can't change your mind, can I?"

"Well, I'll listen. But right now, probably not. You, all the Ruby Sisters, need to hear her story first. Then we need to figure out what is actually going on and if we can help. If not, we'll ask her to move on."

"Okay. I'll go back to the gallery to get my car. I'll see you at your house in a few."

"And I'll call everyone else and have them come over for dinner. That way, we can tell the story to everyone at the same time."

Cindy reached up and hugged Judith, surprising them both.

"Whatever you decide, Judith, I'll help you with it. I just hope you are doing the right thing."

"Me too," Judith said, and reached for her phone.

The phone call found April, legs outstretched in an empty living room, thinking about food and reaching for the phone, hoping that's what Judith wanted too.

Bree and Marsha were returning from the woods, having just made plans to walk in the woods together at least once a week. They had something in common they could help each other with. They were both returning to Spring Falls and trying to find their footing in a new life. Bree wanted someone to talk her stories through, missing Paul and his help, and Marsha needed someone to talk about what she was going to do with the rest of her life.

When their phones rang at the same time, they looked at each other and mouthed, "Judith?" And then realized she had face-timed April too.

"What's wrong?" they all asked at the same time.

"Why does something have to be wrong?" Judith huffed and then, seeing three worried faces, assured them that there was nothing wrong, but she did need their help with something.

"Dinner at my house in an hour?" she asked. "Could one of you pick up a few pizzas?"

"I will," Bree said. She didn't need to ask what everyone wanted. They'd been ordering pizzas together since high school.

After assuring everyone once again that she was fine, Judith hung up and, leaning back against the wall, took a deep breath. She had hedged the truth. Something was wrong. But since it didn't involve any of them personally, it would be okay.

However, she didn't want to, and couldn't really help Nicky by herself. And yes, Cindy was right. It was crazy to bring this stranger into her house, but she saw no other way.

And now, since they were having dinner together, maybe it was the perfect opportunity to let the cat out of the bag about her and Bruce's growing friendship. She suspected they already knew, which made it even more important to bring it out into the open.

She didn't know where their friendship would lead, maybe to nothing. But she loved that she and Bruce were becoming best friends. If something happened from there, she had to admit that was okay with her, which was a gigantic step for her.

But right now, she had a sobbing woman in her office. Nicky had started crying and didn't show any signs of stopping. Nancy had brought her a box of tissues, told her to drink a lot of water, suspecting part of the problem was dehydration.

Judith thought that was true. Dehydration, combined with the relief of telling someone about her sister and asking for help, had probably caused the collapse. Perhaps they could help, maybe they couldn't, but at least they could try.

Lying on the couch, trying to control her sobbing, Nicky tried to make sense of what was happening. She thought she was being moved to Judith's house. It wasn't what she wanted, was it? Just thinking about what it all meant started her sobbing again.

Fear for what she thought she knew, and sorrow for bringing it to these people who didn't really need to know. But she'd done it now. She'd come and stirred everyone's life. They just didn't know it yet. She thought that was what she wanted. Now, she wasn't so sure.

Twenty One

"How was your day?" Mary asked Seth as he took off his boots at the door and reached for Rho.

He had been looking forward all day to the moment he'd hold his new daughter, while pulling his wife close and kissing her cheek. All the baby smells would envelop him and he'd feel as if he'd stepped into his own personal heaven.

It amazed Seth he had gotten so lucky in his life. If all he ever achieved was a happy life with Mary and Rho, he considered himself blessed. But now, he had a chance to fulfill another dream. Becoming his own boss. Mary's friends were amazing, always looking for a way to help the two of them. And that included her birth mother, Bree, who was responsible for Mary's increased happiness.

When he and Mary had first met, Mary didn't even know she was adopted. She thought her mother, Nora, was her birth mother. Seth knew that Mary and Nora had a strange life together, moving around, changing names, but Mary had thought nothing of it. Nora was totally engaged in her daughter's life, and although Mary had to get used to meeting new people every few years, she had come to see it as an adventure.

In fact, it was that last move that had brought them together. If Nora hadn't moved back to Pittsfield and Mary hadn't taken her mother out to lunch that one day at that one time, it was possible that she and Seth would never have met and all this happiness would just be a dream for him.

Mary told him later that they had never been to that restaurant before. She and her mom wanted to try something new. For Seth, it was divine intervention that had sent them there.

Seth knew he'd never forget that day. Ever. He was part of a construction crew working in the building next door, and had been sent over to pick up food for the guys. As he turned away from the counter, he bumped into the woman behind him by mistake, spilling part of a milkshake on her.

She had laughed, and the hostess had brought napkins and everyone had dabbed at her sleeve where the shake had landed.

"Good thing it was vanilla," she had said, and laughed again.

He had been so embarrassed he hadn't taken the time to look at her, but when he did, he stepped back, his face flaming. Later, he knew he had stopped breathing for a moment. But at the time, all he could see was a pair of deep brown eyes twinkling at him, and he knew, just knew, that she was the one. Which rendered him even more speechless.

She had taken pity on him, and said, "Honestly, it's nothing. Don't worry."

And then his heart took over his mouth, and he said, "Can I take you to dinner?"

For a moment, he hoped the earth would open up and swallow him whole. The hostess and her mother stared at him as if he had sprouted horns. But Mary only paused for a moment before saying, "Yes, please."

The hostess tore off a piece of paper from her pad, took down Mary's phone number, and handed it to him. Later, Mary had told him that after he left, the hostess had assured her that Seth was okay. He was a regular at the restaurant, treated everyone kindly, and besides, her brother had gone to school with him so he wasn't too much of a weirdo. Which was why, when he called a few hours later to set up the dinner, Mary had said yes again.

And continued to say yes as they met, talked, learned about their lives, and then, hardly worrying at all, started planning their lives together.

That had been magical enough for any lifetime, Seth thought. But then, a friend on the construction crew told him about work in a town called Spring Falls and said there was a place for him on a construction crew there. Did he want it?

He and Mary had talked it over. Nora had passed away not long after they met, but first she had revealed to Mary that she was adopted. Mary said it didn't matter, Nora was her mom, and left it at that.

But the timing was perfect. A new job meant a new life, and that seemed good to both of them, so they moved to Spring Falls. He started work in the crew his friend had found, and Mary took a job as a waitress at ParaTi.

Her skill learned over years of making new friends wherever she went kicked in immediately. Mary met Judith, and then Cindy, and became friends with them enough that both of them came to their wedding six months after moving to Spring Falls.

Because of her friendship with Judith and Cindy, Mary was there when all the Ruby Sisters returned to Spring Falls, never suspecting for a moment that her birth mother was one of them.

And that was when the next miracle happened. Bree was looking for her daughter, and Mary had decided to look for her birth mother when she got pregnant. A DNA test revealed the truth. It was another Spring Falls magic moment. And now he was ready to tell her how, once again, the Ruby Sisters were going to change their lives for the better.

As he hugged Mary and Rho, Seth answered Mary's question, "Something awesome happened today."

Over a spaghetti dinner with garlic bread made just the way he loved it, Rho settled beside him fast asleep in her swinging chair, Seth told Mary about what happened at the art gallery, and then at April's house.

Mary, her deep brown eyes that held tiny green hazel flecks, sparkled as she listened and asked questions. What did April want to do with the house? Who was filming it? When were they starting? What did April's husband Ron say about it? Did he care how much money April spent? And of course, would Judith's company handle the bookkeeping and taxes?

And then, she asked, "What are you going to call your company, Seth?"

Glancing down at Rho, he said, "It would be weird to call it Rho's Dad Construction, wouldn't it?"

Mary laughed. "Probably, but I can see the tag line as 'I trust him, you can, too.'"

By the end of the night, they had not come up with anything better and settled for R.D. Construction until they could come up with another name.

While Seth fed Rho and got her ready for bed, Mary took a few minutes to write a little more in her book. It was strange how she always wanted to be a writer and then discovered that it was what her mother did. Mary wondered what her father did.

She didn't know who he was and Bree said she had no plans to tell her. Which meant she would just have to trust that Bree knew best and let it go. If she needed to know, then someday she would. Otherwise, it wasn't important. That's what she told herself, anyway.

Twenty Two

April was the first to arrive at Judith's. She had left her car at Judith's that morning since Ron had taken her to the house, and after that she had walked, so she had to call a ride service. While she waited for her ride, she fretted, not knowing why. A wave of worry had washed over her when Judith called, and she couldn't make it go away.

Although Judith had said that there was nothing to worry about, that didn't feel like the truth. So by the time she stepped out of the car, April had already imagined several scenarios of what could be wrong. She stood in the driveway and tried to calm down, told herself that everything was fine and let herself in the front door with her key.

Dropping her keys in her purse, hanging up her coat, and shedding her shoes, she paused in the foyer and said a brief prayer of gratitude for Judith's warm home. Soon she'd have to move out and into her own home and she'd miss not having someone to live with, since Ron would be gone most of the time.

"We're in here," Judith called out.

Since she had seen no other cars in the driveway, April wondered who the "we" could be. Stepping into the living room, April was startled to see a strange woman sitting on Judith's couch, with Judith hovering over her as if she might break or was a stray animal she had brought home, and wasn't sure what it would do next.

For some reason, a ray of fear sliced through April and she took a step back, her hand going to her heart in surprise. Floating in front of the fear were questions. Was she supposed to know this woman? Why was she here? It was totally irrational of her, but something made her think that this woman was dangerous. But if she was, why was she in Judith's house? Judith knew better than that!

Judith stepped over to April, blocking her view of the woman, and holding both her hands, asked, "Are you alright?"

April's heart was racing and felt as if she was gasping for breath, but Judith's strong and confident presence helped. "Maybe," she answered. "Why wouldn't I be? But who is that?"

Judith squinted at April and April knew Judith knew that she really wasn't okay, but she was trying to get there. Why she was upset was a question they'd have to deal with later. Both of them knew something had triggered that reaction, and being Judith, she wouldn't be able to leave it alone.

For now, though, she kept holding on to April's hands and smiled down at her as she answered. "Her name is Nicky. We'll talk about the reason I brought her home after everyone gets here. Do you want to come in now, or wait?"

April took another step back as she answered. "I'll wait. I'll change clothes and be right back."

Upstairs, as April passed the spare bedroom, she saw a purse sitting on the bed, and another slice of fear ran through her. It was so irrational that she became even more afraid. What was wrong with her? How could this woman be dangerous? She looked like a scared cat that had come out of the rain.

But after the high she had experienced at her new house with Seth and the joy she felt thinking how she would transform the house into something spectacular, the drop into fear and anxiety was shocking.

There was nothing about the woman that should cause fear. If anything, it should have triggered her mothering response. Maybe it was because something about the woman felt familiar. And then she remembered. She had bumped into her earlier that day.

At first, that memory seemed to calm the fear because it gave her a reason for her response. It was because of the coincidence of seeing her twice in one day. But as April sat on the bed, changing into a pair of warm sweatpants, she realized that made her even more uneasy. Did the woman bump into her on purpose? And how did she worm her way into Judith's house?

"We're here!" Bree called up. "And I have pizza! Come and get it!"

The sound of Bree's voice immediately made April feel better. She had just spent a lovely day with all her friends, had decided to start her own little design business in a beautiful new home, and now they were all together, safe and secure.

That fear she had felt was unfounded. There was nothing to worry about.

• • • ● ● • ● ● • •

Nicky took one look at April standing in the doorway and wanted to run. She couldn't do this. She couldn't tell the story and turn that woman's life upside down. It wasn't her fault. Besides, she could be wrong about the whole thing.

She started to get up off the couch, ready to get herself out of town before anything bad happened, but Judith's look pinned her down and she stopped. And then the front door opened, and Bree's cheerful voice rang out, and it was too late.

When Bree and Marsha came into the living room, they stared at her in the same way that April had done. But there was no fear. Just curiosity.

But then, of course, it wasn't their lives that would turn upside down if she was right, Nicky thought.

Although the entire reason she had come to Spring Falls was for vengeance, after meeting Judith, and seeing that Judith would, and could, help, the urge to destroy had fallen away. Now she was just terrified. And a huge part of her prayed that what she had discovered would affect none of these women.

All she really wanted was to find out what happened to her sister. And if someone had done something to her, stop him from hurting someone else. Because Nicky knew that someone was doing something to many women—not just her sister. And that someone had passed through Spring Falls and lived there for a time.

Reminding herself that she was there to help save others from who this man was, eased her conscious. Not much, but enough to give a small smile to the women in front of her, and when April joined them, she could smile at her, too.

April tilted her head, thinking perhaps that she was more tired than she had thought and had overreacted. With all her friends around, her life was good and they could help this woman. Whoever she was. Judith had brought her to the house for a reason. It had to be a good one.

They set pizza on the coffee table, added paper plates and napkins. Bree had gotten everyone what they wanted from the refrigerator before Judith said, "This is Nicky Blair. Nicky has been searching for her sister for most of her life. And we are going to help Nicky find her."

No one questioned why. If Judith said they were, they were.

Bree took a slice of pizza, tucked her feet up under her, and said, "Well, then, I guess we better hear the whole story."

Twenty Three

B ooker Nathan Morris was embarrassed and ashamed of himself. He should know better. He hadn't intended to do this, but then after all these years, there she was in the pizza shop. The same one they all used to go to. How many years ago? At least a few lifetimes.

He had been so shocked at seeing her, he had followed her. Now he was parked outside of the pretty two story home with all the lights blazing in the living room and wondering what to do.

It had taken him a moment to realize that the other two women who had also gone inside were women he also knew. *What had they called themselves in high school?* Some kind of stone sisters. It made them all a little hard to get to know, because they were always together.

He had been afraid of them all then. If you liked one, you better like them all, or at least win all of them over. And he didn't know how to do that. And he had his own issues, so he had acted like a jerk and broke up with her.

I was just a teenager, Booker thought, running his hand through his hair. He still had his hair—gone gray now—but still there. That was the only good thing he had going for him. And his work. Somehow he had managed to end up doing something with his life that he loved doing.

Everything else had fallen away. The woman he married too young had divorced him after years of him neglecting her and had taken their children with her. Now they were grown, and called him dad when they called to check up on him, even though they had grown up with another man.

Small blessings, Booker said to himself.

All of it had been his fault, and he knew it. He had spent the years after the divorce trying to make up for his piss-poor behavior by working to bring a measure of peace and safety to his hometown of Spring Falls. That had worked, at least. Even if his home life hadn't.

Although he had dated after the divorce, nothing stuck. The job made him always on call. He was not someone you could count on to sustain any kind of relationship. So he had given up. Love was for others. not for him. And he was content to leave it that way.

And then, cruising the streets, he had seen a woman in the pizza shop who looked a lot like that girl he had once loved. Not that he knew that then, or told her. He had done the exact opposite.

But now he tried to tell the truth to himself, and he knew he had lost his heart to her at sixteen and then promptly broke hers, along with his, because he was—as he said so many times to himself—stupid.

Young, I was young, he muttered to himself, trying, and failing, to feel better about what he had done back then.

He had slowed down, watched the woman, and then realized that it really was her. After all these years. Questions flooded his brain. Why was she in town? Where had she been? What was she doing buying pizza?

And because his profession was about getting answers, he followed her. And now he was sitting, like a stalker, outside this pleasant house, in a quiet neighborhood, wondering what to do next. Be brave and walk up to the door, ring the doorbell and say hi? How was he going to explain how he ended up in front of this house?

But then the matter was taken out of his hands. The front door opened and out walked the woman the entire town both loved and feared. Including him. They had fought both together and against each other at many a town hall meeting.

He had never asked her what happened to her friends. They had continued on with their public lives, never becoming friends themselves. Both their choices. She blamed him, and he blamed himself.

Booker watched Judith pause on the porch, her red hair lit up with the light from the hallway and Booker prayed she would stay where she was, just wave him on, and go back into the house. It was a legend in town that if Judith's red hair flared for a minute, someone was in trouble.

Of course, it was just the hall light that made it look that way, Booker said to himself.

But then she stepped off the porch and headed across the lawn directly to his car. *Too late to leave now.* Trying desperately to come up with a reason he was parked across the street from Judith's house, he thought he would just say he had stopped to make a call.

Judith knocked on his window. Pressing the button, he lowered the window, and realized there was no point in lying to this woman. He'd have to tell her the truth.

"What are you doing out here, Booker?" Judith asked. But before he could say anything, she waved her hand and said, "Never mind. It must be fate. Come on in. A woman is about to tell a story that you probably need to hear."

When he hesitated, Judith correctly assessed why. "What are you, still a teenage boy with a crush? Afraid to say you were an idiot? Yes, Bree is inside. You can apologize to her later. Right now we have a bigger problem than that you are still in love with high-school Bree."

"This is why people are afraid of you, Judith," Booker said, getting out of the car. "You say things like that."

"Why Booker Morris, are you telling me that you are afraid of me?" Judith laughed, hooking her hand around his arm.

"Yes, ma'am," Booker said. "Always have been."

"Oh," Judith said, stopping in the middle of the yard to look at him directly. "You were afraid of us? Now that is something I hadn't thought of. Well, don't be afraid now. At least not of us. I think we have a much bigger problem to solve, and we need you, Mr. Police Chief, to hear this story and see what you think."

"It's worse than facing Bree and the rest of you, whatever-you-call-yourself-sisters?"

"Ruby Sisters, and yes, if it's true, it's much worse."

Twenty Four

R on took his time finishing his drink, sipping it, savoring the feel as it slipped down his throat. As he drank, Ron closed his eyes and thought about his next trip. As he imagined the possibilities, Ron decided he didn't need to wait another day to leave. The office ran smoothly without him. They were used to him going away. He had two managers that he trusted to make money while he was gone and manage the underlings, so that wasn't a problem.

He could text them in the morning and let them know some out-of-town business had come up, and he needed to take care of it. None of them questioned where he went or why. If they wanted their jobs, and the benefits he provided, they knew to keep their questions to themselves. He was a good, kind, generous, if illusive owner.

Besides, Ron knew they not only didn't mind when he took his trips, they secretly liked it. He was a meticulous boss. Everything had to run the way he wanted it to, and he could feel the edge of fear his being in the office generated. So he kept his working in the office to a minimum, not wanting to upset the harmony that generated the lifestyle he and April enjoyed.

He didn't have to explain anything to April. She was not there, happy now in Spring Falls. And although he had resented it at first, now he understood how much it benefited him.

And Ron realized, with a start, he knew where he wanted to go next. It was a place he could drive to instead of flying. He'd enjoy that. As long as a winter storm didn't come in, he'd be gone only a few days at the most. He hadn't been to the town for years, and years, and he wondered how much it had changed since the last time he had done business there.

Yes, Ron decided. *I need this trip.* Washing his glass, and putting the few things he had used away, Ron headed upstairs to the bedroom to pack. He loved the process of getting ready for his trips almost as much as he loved the trips themselves.

The anticipation of what he would find was like something he could almost taste: sweet, sour, and spicy. And preparation for travel brought him a calmness that he experienced no other time. It was an unbeatable combination.

As Ron packed, he took pleasure in what he was doing, like folding the clothes he would take with him. They were the same ones he always wore, but something about putting them into the suitcase made him happy. He had cubes for each type of clothing; one for his shirts, one for pants, belts. Everything he needed. Easy to unpack or keep them the way they were.

Neat. Arranged just so. His way. No one else's. For a moment, Ron flashed back to his chaotic childhood. The mess, the noise, the uncertainly. But the smooth coolness of the fabric in his hands as he folded brought him back to his life now, where everything was under control.

It was his world, all his. No noise. No poverty. No throwing of dishes, or cursing, or fists pounding, or yelling. None of that, anymore. He had the life he wanted. Peaceful and quiet. And he would never let that kind of chaos touch the life he had now.

Putting each cube into his suitcase, he smiled. Everything spoke of calm elegance. The cube's color was just slightly grayer than the inside lining of the suitcase, and spoke of his elegant taste. It was perfect. Better than the one April had taken with her.

When he had to buy a new suitcase, he splurged and bought himself the best he could find. The wheels rolled with a smooth precision, and it was so light it was easy to lift into an overhead bin when he flew.

He remembered the moment he realized April had taken his suitcase. Not only did that mean she had left him, but she had taken something she couldn't ever know about. He had hidden a few things he needed for his trips behind the lining. But they were so lightweight she wouldn't have felt the difference and would never have thought to look there. Still, he had been an idiot, and he had been terrified that somehow she might have found them.

But she hadn't, and he had removed the items the first chance he got, breathing a sigh of relief, determined to not be so foolish again. So there were no hidden places in this suitcase. He had found a better method of taking what he needed. In fact, because of that brief scare, he had changed his style of travel. Travel lighter.

The world was so different from when he had first begun taking these trips. On one hand, it was more complicated, with all the cameras and cell phones and GPS and cookies on computers. On the other hand, it was easier to get what he wanted. *It was a give and take,* Ron decided. And since technology had made him rich, it was not something he was going to rail against. He'd embrace it.

Thinking of April, Ron thought about calling her before he left. She didn't need to know he would be traveling and would be out of touch for a while, but he had discovered that he missed her, and he wanted to see her face before he left.

But it was late, and she would probably be in bed. And if he left as early as he planned, he would wake her up. *Oh well,* Ron thought. *We talked earlier. And she's happy about the house.* He'd speak to her when he got back, maybe come home through Spring Falls, if all went well.

Laying out the clothes he would wear in the morning, Ron slipped into bed, feeling the silkiness of the sheets, and let himself dream about where he was going, and the work that he would do there. His life was exactly how he wanted it to be, and it filled him with gratitude for whatever deity had made it happen for him.

Twenty Five

"Look who's here," Judith said, pulling Booker into the living room.

There was an audible gasp and then a dead silence while everyone waited for someone else to say something.

It was Cindy who broke the spell, giving the embarrassed Booker a hug. As he bent over to hug her back, he whispered, "Thank you."

In all his life, Booker had never imagined a more embarrassing moment. But with Cindy standing close beside him, he realized it was also a moment of happiness, because except for the stranger sitting on the sofa, these were people he knew.

It didn't matter that he hadn't seen three of them for almost thirty years. They had history together. He felt at home in this room, and that both surprised and delighted him.

Cindy held his hand as they crossed the room and gestured to an empty chair beside her. She and Booker had seen each other around town, and he had stopped by the gallery once in a while to say hello, so even though they couldn't call each other best friends, he wasn't a stranger to her.

Both she and Judith had supported Booker's campaign to be Police Chief. Except for the dumping of their best friend in high school, Booker had always seemed to them to be a loyal and good man.

They knew about his marriage, and divorce, and his unsuccessful attempts at dating. Sometimes Cindy and Judith would wonder what would have happened if Bree had never met Paul. Would she and Booker have gotten together again once they were both more mature?

And now Bree and Booker were both in the same room after all these years, and the spark of energy that flew across the room between them was hard to ignore, even though the two of them were doing their best not to notice each other.

"Sorry for interrupting your meeting," Booker said, hands still on his thighs, trying to act like the Police Chief that he was and not a nervous sixteen-year-old.

"How did you happen to be here?" Marsha asked, suspecting she was putting him on the spot, and liking that she was.

"Well," Booker said, clearing his throat. "I saw a woman who looked like Bree, and then I realized it was actually Bree, and I was so shocked I followed her. Sorry about that.

"But geez, Bree," he said, finally looking directly at Bree, "It gave me a start to see you here. I had no idea you were in town. And then I saw Cindy and Marsha and I couldn't imagine how you were all in town and I didn't know it. So, yes, Judith saw me lurking outside and invited me in. Once again, sorry about that!"

Marsha laughed. "Kinda embarrassing, isn't it?"

"You could say that." Booker said, looking down. "But Judith said there was something I needed to hear?"

"It's something everyone needs to hear," Judith said, gesturing at Nicky, who had been doing her best to disappear. "I just met

Nicky Blair today. She told me a story, and I realized we might be able to help her."

When everyone turned their attention to Nicky, she dropped her head and mumbled, "I don't know if I can do that."

Once again, it was Cindy who understood. "This must be exceptionally hard for you, Nicky. You don't know us. We don't know you, and the story you want tell us must be a hard story to tell. Let's eat first, and catch up with Booker, and that might help you be more comfortable."

"Pizza's in the dining room," Judith said, grateful for Cindy's tact.

Bree stood, not sure what to do next. Everyone, except Nicky, knew that Booker was the boy who had broken her heart. It had mended, and she had met Paul and would never have traded her life with Paul for a life with Booker. But she knew she was still carrying at least a little anger at how he had ended their relationship.

Still, the rational part of her thought it was ridiculous. They were kids then. Now they were adults. Grown-ups. And she was a grandmother, for heaven's sake. All of that swept through her thoughts as Booker stood and headed towards her, thinking it was best to get it over with.

"Since I am sorry for breaking into your meeting, could I add another sorry to that?"

Reaching out, he grabbed one of Bree's hands as he said, "I am sorry that my past self was such an idiot and treated you with such disrespect."

Bree looked up into the blue eyes that had captured her attention so long ago, and saw the gentle and kind boy she had once known, and smiled.

"We were both idiots. And I've been an idiot many times since. Someday, perhaps you can tell me what happened, but otherwise, let's move on."

"Stories to share?" Booker asked, still holding her hand.

"Stories to share, but not now. Another time."

Booker nodded. "I am looking forward to it."

Across the room, Judith watched the exchange and smiled to herself. But then she looked at Nicky, whose hands were trembling as she picked at her pizza and she felt that bolt of fear again.

Nicky's story affected them all somehow. She was sure of that. But how? That, she didn't know, and she almost wished that she wouldn't have to find out. Almost. But as always, Judith knew secrets destroyed. And it was better to bring them into the open instead of letting them fester, causing unseen and yet devastating disasters.

Judith caught April's eyes and realized that April was more afraid than she was. Did she know something about Nicky and her story, or was she being sensitive to how Nicky was feeling?

Reaching out and pulling her close, Judith whispered, "What's wrong?"

"I don't know, really. It just feels as if there is something terrifying lurking in the shadows. It's irrational, I know, but still...."

"It's okay. I feel it too. But we have each other. Whatever it is, it can't destroy that."

April nodded and leaned into Judith, grateful for her strength. Nevertheless, to herself, she said, *I hope that's true.*

Twenty Six

Cindy opened the back door to her gallery, hoping she could slip in unnoticed. But Mimi spotted her immediately, opened her mouth to say a cheery hello and then stopped and stared.

"What the blazes is going on?" Mimi asked instead. But when Cindy flinched and she realized how abrupt that was, asked more gently, "What's wrong? Are you well? Did something happen?"

Like Judith, Mimi tended to go after something with a vengeance. She was fiercely protective of her wife, Janet, and anyone she counted as a friend. And although Cindy was her employer, and they both knew their roles, they had also become friends. Not like Ruby Sister friends. The next layer of friends is how Mimi thought of it.

When Cindy just stood there looking confused, Mimi got worried.

"You are scaring me, Cindy. Really, are you okay? Should I call Judith, or April or ...?"

"No, I'm okay. Besides, they probably look the same as me."

Seeing Mimi's puzzled face, she added, "We were up late. I'll be okay. Just let me get settled and let's meet about our plans for the holiday party."

When Cindy emerged from her office an hour later, some of the frazzled look was gone. She had meant to get some work done, but ended up falling asleep with her head on her arms at her desk. Now she wanted coffee and carbohydrates.

She had barely slept the night before. Hearing Nicky's story about her missing sister Sarah had bothered Cindy so much her stomach and head started hurting. Ignoring how she felt, she had moved to sit beside Nicky with her arm around her, hoping that would give her strength.

It didn't matter that they had just met that day. Nicky needed help, and Cindy knew how to give it. That kind of help wasn't something she tried to make herself do. It was who she was. She couldn't stop herself, even though Judith had told her countless times to take care of herself first.

But last night it had to be done, even if today it felt as if Nicky had pulled half of her energy out of Cindy's body. And then not sleeping well had removed even more. Cindy knew she shouldn't let herself get so drained, but how could she not have helped?

Hearing Cindy move around in the back room, Janet poked her head in and asked if Cindy wanted her to run to the coffee shop and bring back some coffee and pastries.

Cindy managed to nod yes while saying, "Yes, please. Come get me when you get back," and went back to her office and put her head down again on her desk. This time, she left the door open. She wasn't fooling anyone. Mimi and Janet wanted to help. She'd let them.

Mittens, seeing the open door, sauntered in and headed straight for Cindy's lap. After kneading a nest, she curled around and settled in gently purring, enough that it put Cindy right back to sleep.

Fifteen minutes later, Cindy woke, feeling much better. It was as if Mittens had transferred some of her own energy to her. Leaning over, she kissed the top of Mittens' head, stood, and put Mittens on the desk chair to get her own rest.

"Feeling better?" Mimi asked as Janet handed out coffees and napkins for the pastries.

"Much, and this helps," Cindy said, gesturing at what Janet had brought. "And I know you are curious about what kept me and the rest of the Ruby Sisters up last night, but if you don't mind, I think we need to keep it private for the time being. Once we know more, we'll probably be wanting your help."

Janet glanced at Mimi with a slight tilt of her head to let her know that it probably was not a good idea to push Cindy right now. Mimi winked in acknowledgment.

"Okay, then, let's talk about the holiday party," Mimi said.

A few hours later, they had a plan. The decorations were already up, thanks to Seth. Mimi said that she checked with their friends who owned the restaurant down the street, and yes, they would cater it. They would speak to the person who managed the website and have them send out an invitation to all of their list, not just the local people. Everyone. Cindy believed in unity, not separation. Even if most of the people on their mailing list lived elsewhere, she would keep them in the loop, giving out small gifts, and providing coupons for holiday shopping.

Of course, all her artists would be invited, and everyone in town, on her mailing list or not. What made her holiday party different, or at least she hoped it did, was it didn't last for just an hour or two. It was all day. Drop in when you can. Stay as long as you wish, or just say hello.

Everyone would leave with a small gift, and everyone was welcome. As they talked, Cindy realized she would need more help. Of course, she could hire Mary for the day, and ask the Ruby Sisters if they could help. And she'd ask Judith to have the bookkeeper spend the day with them—in case they had orders, she could handle that part while the staff took care of the people.

"Why not have April co-ordinate the look of all of this?" Mimi asked.

"Great idea," Cindy responded. And thought that not only was it a great idea for the gallery, but also for April. After hearing Nicky's story, April looked as if someone had hit her with a baseball bat. Stunned. Not herself.

Of course, it had devastated them all to learn of Nicky's past. Who wouldn't feel upset at hearing it? But April seemed the most disturbed. But then, Bree had too. At the time Cindy had put Bree's over-reaction down to being uncomfortable at seeing Booker again, but now she wondered.

There was something about Nicky and her sister that meant trouble for all of them. She couldn't figure out what that might be, but for some reason, it seemed both April and Bree felt it the most.

Twenty Seven

B ree didn't even bother to get up the next morning. She woke up, rolled over and said to herself, *No.*

Not only was she tired from the long night and restless sleep, she also didn't want to deal with the day. So she did something she hadn't done since Paul died. She remained buried beneath blankets, pretending that nothing had changed.

Besides, she said to herself, *it's miserable out there.*

She could tell. Peaking out from her blankets, she had a view of her tiny backyard. She had it completely fenced in, and she had motion sensor lights and cameras installed, so she felt safe leaving her curtains open at night. She enjoyed being able to see a patch of night sky as she fell asleep.

This morning she could see the wind whipping the limbs of the maple tree and little white flakes of snow swirling among the branches. The first snow of winter. *Blah,* she said to herself. It was a great day to not get up.

The book she was writing, which usually pulled her out of bed in the morning, was silent. Sometimes she had ideas of what to write next, but often it was simply the joy of spending time in a world she had made up.

Although she had ideas about what the book was about, mostly she wrote like a reader. Surprised to see what her characters were doing, and what the plot line was twisting around to be.

As she listened to that poor woman tell her story last night, Bree thought of it like a book. What was the theme? What was the plot line? What was true, and what wasn't? She knew she was listening to the story, as if it had not really happened, because it was so hard to hear.

And then there was Booker. She hadn't seen him since their high-school graduation, and then only across the rows of chairs as they waited for their names to be called. With the last name of Curtis, she was called before him and she had been aware of how his gaze had followed her. But when his name was called, she didn't look, still hurt from his rejection.

But last night, with no warning, he had walked into Judith's living room. And this time she couldn't help but look. He was a man now. Heavier, grayer, and more at ease with himself, but then weren't they all? Bree wished Booker had aged badly and then berated herself for the thought.

She wouldn't wish that on anyone, and she only wished it because there was that little twinge of excitement at seeing him that she used to get when she glimpsed him at his locker, or when he would wait for her after school to walk her home.

It had been a brief puppy-love romance, and they had gone their separate ways. Supposedly, they had both agreed to it. That was the story they told. But what was true was he had dumped her, and she had never really forgiven him. Mostly because she never understood why.

And Bree was fully aware that when she declared the hunky professor, Paul Stanford Mann, as her future husband, the fact that he looked a little like Booker had made her look twice.

Groaning, Bree rolled over and pulled the covers tighter around her, trying to make a warm snuggly cocoon for herself. It worked for another hour, and then the combination of hunger and the bathroom nudged her awake again. She still didn't want to get up, because she knew that once she did, she would have to deal with all the feelings that came up last night.

Not just the ones around the memory of the past and Booker, but also the fear that somehow Nicky's story would change all their lives, and change, although often good in the end, was always hard. Always. And she had been through enough of that to last her a lifetime.

As Bree swung her legs over the side of the bed in preparation for getting up, which took longer each day than she thought it should, she realized something. She would say yes to the offer to buy this house. She had been renting, but the owners wanted to move to Florida and didn't want to deal with a house. They would put it on the market unless she wanted to buy it.

She had asked them to give her some time to think about it. When she first came home to Spring Falls, her intention was to stay only a short time. But now her daughter and granddaughter lived in Spring Falls too, and she never wanted to be apart from them again.

Bree also knew that the spark that made her finally decide to buy the house and stay was seeing Booker again. She hated to admit it, but there it was. And after Booker had left, Judith had told the group a little of his life story, so Bree knew he was single like her. Just the thought made her feel disloyal to Paul.

And as she had taken to doing, she asked Paul what she should do. It was just her pretending that he was still around, but it helped

117

with the sorrow of not seeing him, and she imagined his answer was he wanted her to have a good and happy life.

After all, that had been his last gift to her, forcing her to face up to her past, find her friends, and then her daughter. And now, perhaps a little companionship too. Bree's face flushed with embarrassment.

That's the last thing I need, she said to herself.

After a shower and coffee, Bree felt better. She would give herself a day off from writing. Perhaps do a little online shopping. When she left her life behind after Paul's death, she took very little of it with her. And that meant she only had a few warm clothes. A few hours later, she had ordered a coat, sweaters, boots, and warmer pants, plus slippers and a heavier quilt for her bed.

When she called the owners, asking them to get the process started on buying the house, they were ecstatic. They wanted to leave their home in good hands, and they were eager to go to Florida, especially now that the snow lay on the ground. Not much, but enough to remind them that they didn't want to spend another winter in the cold.

Bree had almost convinced herself that there was nothing going on that bothered her when her phone pinged and brought her back to earth. A message from Judith. Could she meet with Booker, Nicky, and herself?

Reluctantly, Bree texted back, *yes.* It had been good to pretend that last night had never happened, but she couldn't stay in that bubble forever. She knew Judith asked her because she would help them think through things logically. She refused to think that Judith had any other motive.

Bree also had to admit that she was glad Judith asked. She had to face Booker eventually, and also there was something in Nicky's story that was bothering her. She didn't know what it could be.

There was no way what happened to Nicky's sister could affect her and the Ruby Sister's lives. And yet, it felt as if it did.

Twenty Eight

J udith had resisted the urge to call Bruce after the meeting. It had been late, he'd be asleep. It wasn't an emergency.

But she wanted to hear his voice, and his calm assurance that Nicky's story would not turn their world upside down. Because even though there were no signs pointing to it affecting any of them, just helping Nicky would make them all question what they knew and what they didn't about people they knew and trusted. That was the way of the world, distrust.

Judith knew that wasn't necessarily a bad thing. It was the intent that mattered, and what determined the outcome. *Always question everything* had been her motto forever. When she learned something, before accepting it, she'd tried to always ask herself, *is it true?*

But she had never asked herself that question about Spring Falls. Was it true that it was a safe place to live? Was it true that nothing terrible ever happened there?

It's why, before Booker left last night, she had set up a meeting with him. She had asked him if he could look up the reports of

Sara's disappearance, and see if what Nicky had told them rang true?

"Would have done it anyway," he had answered.

Now that it was morning, and she had slept well despite a mind churning with ideas, Judith texted Bruce and asked if he had time to talk. He called immediately, and Judith felt herself sinking comfortably into the sound of his voice.

She had stopped resisting that she loved talking to him. The first time she saw him on a Zoom call, when she called him about Paul's letter, her response to seeing him had shocked her.

Never in a zillion years would she have thought herself capable, let alone willing, to experience what people call love at first sight. And even now, she would not admit that they had a romantic love relationship.

No. They had a companion relationship, and yes, that was love to her. And she suspected that was how he felt, too. Eventually, they'd have to talk about it, but for now, this was how she wanted it to be.

"What's up?"

"Do you have time for a fairly long story?"

"I'll make time. Give me a sec."

A minute later, he was back on the phone. Judith knew he had just handed his secretary whatever work he had been planning to do himself.

"Okay, what's the story?"

For the next hour, Judith ran everything by Bruce that Nicky had told them. He listened carefully, asked questions when necessary, and when she was done, asked her the two questions she had asked herself.

"Do you believe her?"

"I don't want to, but I do."

"And does that mean you are going to do whatever you can to help?"

"Yes, that's what it means."

"Well, Judith, that means I will too. Just let me know what you need."

"You've given it to me, Bruce. And I will keep you up to date. Perhaps you will see something I don't."

After hanging up, Judith spent a moment thanking Paul once again for the gift he had given her when he had hired Bruce as the estate attorney that would handle his last wishes. She knew it wasn't possible for Paul to hear her, but she did it anyway, just in case.

Then she texted Bree to come to the meeting with Booker. Yes, she needed Bree's clear thinking, but she admitted to herself that she was also interested in seeing how Booker and Bree would work together.

Admit it, Judith said to herself. *You're playing matchmaker.*

Never, she answered herself, and then smiled. Of course she was. Booker was alone, and so was Bree. All she was doing was putting together what was obvious.

She hoped figuring out what happened to Sara would be as easy.

If Booker would have known that Bree was going to be at the meeting with Judith, too, he might have canceled. Instead, he got up early and began planning how he would research Nicky's story. It bothered him that he was excited about what Nicky had shared. Not excited about what happened to her sister, but that it was a puzzle to solve.

Although he loved how orderly and planned out his days were, this mystery added an element of excitement, giving him something more than spending each day managing a small police station.

And although he was called the Police Chief, it didn't mean he had a police force. He had three full-time officers and a few part-time ones he could call in for special events like Fourth of July parades.

There wasn't really a need for more than that. It was a small, quiet town. Their primary job as a police force was keeping the trafficking of drugs out of town and away from the schools. And of course, the routine traffic accidents, speeding tickets, and sometimes domestic abuse calls.

He loved the job. And now he had a mystery to solve. The only tie to his town was that Nicky said that the person she suspected had lived here at some point. The problem was, she didn't say who that was and no amount of prying got it out of her.

Nicky had told Booker to do what she had done. Find out who was in Jakestown when Sara went missing, and who also lived in Spring Falls for a time,

"Makes no sense, Nicky," he had said.

"It does," she had answered. "Look and see if any other girls or women went missing from Spring Falls. You have the database. I just went from town to town asking people for years. You'll find it faster. But I promise you that the answer you will find is that there is an overlapping person. And when you tell me that person's name, I'll tell you if it's the person I found, too."

Booker agreed. He'd check. He had never heard of anyone gone missing.

"It was a long time ago," she said. "Besides, you know how people just say that girls run away? Well, that's not always true, is it? I'll give you a hint. Look at the years 1985-1989."

When Booker heard those years, he realized he knew someone who had disappeared during that time. It was someone from their high school. At the memory, he had glanced around the room to see if any of the Ruby Sisters remembered.

None of them reacted. Were they good actresses, or did they not know? He'd find out. Everyone had said she moved away. But what if that wasn't what happened?

A few hours later, he had a few answers and more questions. He gathered up the papers, grabbed his phone, and headed out the door to meet Judith.

Twenty Nine

Even though Judith was trying to be quiet, April could hear the murmur of her voice, and from the way she was speaking, April knew she had to be talking to Bruce.

She's probably running last night's meeting by him, April thought. And then rolled over and pulled a pillow over her head so she wouldn't be tempted to listen.

Plus, she felt overwhelmed. Yesterday had been a day filled with a wide range of changes, ideas, and emotions.

First seeing the house with Ron and wondering how she could learn to like it. Then saying goodbye to him, not knowing when he'd be back.

After that, she spent time with Bree and baby Rho and gained a sense of calm as she breathed in Rho's baby scent. Then the gallery and the decision with Seth to start a small business together designing houses, starting with hers.

All of that would have been enough to last her for days, but then that woman Nicky came along and they had their emergency meeting. And to top it all off, Booker showed up.

April felt as if she had been on a roller coaster all day, and the world was still spinning from the open possibilities of everything that had happened. Part of her wanted to stay in bed and the other part wanted to spring up and take over the world.

Then, to her surprise, she started to cry. Hearing the murmur of Judith's voice had revealed to her how much she wanted someone like Bruce to talk to. *Wouldn't a normal person be able to call their husband and discuss the day?* But that had never been part of her and Ron's relationship. He controlled the when and where of their conversations.

If he called her, they could talk. But he wouldn't. In fact, for all she knew, he wasn't even at their house in Silver Lake right now. And even if he was there, if she called, he wouldn't answer. He'd check in with her when he wanted to. He'd show up at their new house when he wanted to.

For the first time, April acknowledged to herself that was not the way a marriage should work. At least not the one that she wanted. Her parents had shown her what communication in a marriage looked like. How had she missed it in hers?

Her parents were always together, and when they weren't, they constantly checked on each other. Equal partners sharing a life, holding hands as they walked. That was not what she and Ron had. They never had it. Except when they were dating, when he was always nearby.

After they married and moved to Silver Lake, he started doing his own thing, showing up when he wanted to. Then the kids came along and her attention went to them.

But he was always so loving and kind when he was with us, April reasoned to herself. Except for the temper tantrum he had thrown that had brought her back to Spring Falls.

And now you have a new life of your own, she said to herself, throwing off the covers. There was a lot to be done with the house.

If Ron wanted to have a life that she wasn't part of, she'd let him. She would make a life of her own. Which meant money of her own. She needed to talk to Judith about how to set up her new business so it would be only hers. She had opened a bank account of her own yesterday. Maybe it was time to move some of the money Ron gave her to that account. Just enough so it wouldn't be obvious.

Standing in the middle of the bedroom, April realized that if she was thinking of doing that, Ron probably had done it ages ago. He had another life. It was so obvious. How could she have missed it? But what was the other life? What did he do when he was gone? How much money had he squirreled away that she didn't know about?

It was useless to berate herself for not realizing it before. It didn't mean he didn't love her. It didn't mean that they didn't have a decent marriage. He did, and they did. But for the first time, she admitted it wasn't enough. Only now that she was in Spring Falls with her friends and with the idea for a life of her own, was she as happy as she had been before meeting Ron.

But then there was that woman, Nicky, April thought. Nicky sleeping in the other bedroom. Nicky with a missing sister. Why had she come into their lives?

There was a hidden reason, and she'd find out what it was. Maybe she'd get to know Nicky better by asking her if she would like to help her with the new house?

Determined now, April pulled on jeans and a sweatshirt, stuck her feet into a pair of bunny slippers Judith had bought her, and headed down the stairs. Judith had made coffee and brought out her cinnamon buns and was just sitting down at the table herself. A plate of fruit was also on the table.

April pointed at it and asked, "An offset to the cinnamon buns?"

"Absolutely," Judith said. "How did you sleep?"

"Well. And not. It was a crazy day yesterday." After taking a sip of coffee, she added, "I was thinking of asking Nicky if she wanted to help me with the house. I'd like to get it up and running enough that I can live there."

Seeing Judith's face, she quickly added, "Not that I haven't loved living here, but I think it's time to get my life together." Then she filled Judith in on what else she wanted to do and asked if she could help her.

Judith smiled, and said, "Helping you set up your business and new life would give me so much pleasure, April. And I think it's a good idea to ask Nicky to help you with the house."

As the two of them clinked their coffee cups together, Judith couldn't help but smile to herself. She was happy Ron wasn't around much. She wanted to like and trust him, and it was hard to admit she never did or had. He could stay away forever as far as she was concerned. As long as April was happy, she was happy.

Thirty

Nicky also heard the murmur of Judith's voice. She wasn't sure who Judith was talking to, but it was probably the man she had seen Judith with in the restaurant. *Good,* she thought, *more people taking over for me.*

Now that she had finally told the story—twice—she felt wrung out and empty, and all she wanted now was to leave. Run as fast as she could to somewhere else. Anywhere else. As long as no one knew her and she could start again.

She had been leaving places for over thirty years, all in the name of searching for Sara. But now that she had this group of people curious enough, they would search until they found her. She could start a new life somewhere. The one she was creating before Sara went missing.

She was a vagabond even then. Now she could be a vagabond searching for adventure, not a sister.

At your age? Nicky said to herself. *Get a grip. Where will you go? And do what?*

As she often did, Nicky heard her sister's voice, this time urging her to stay.

"You're right," Nicky said to the sister who lived in her head. "I might as well finish what I started."

Nicky looked around the bedroom that Judith had given her. It was nicer than most places she had lived in. And it was free. For now, anyway. But she needed to find a job. Maybe Judith, who seemed to know everyone, could help her. Or maybe one of the other women. While they still pitied her, and before they started hating her.

As Nicky dressed to go downstairs, she thought of how each of them had listened to her story. Judith, along with Booker, seemed to see it as a puzzle that they were determined to solve. Bree kept moving around. Was she restless or upset? Marsha kept looking away. But that might have been from something other than her story. Marsha seemed almost as lost as her. Nicky wondered what that was about.

Cindy kept sending her sympathetic looks, and afterward it was Cindy who hugged her and said it would be okay, even though both of them knew it wouldn't be.

And then there was April. She appeared interested and ready to help, but at the same time, suspicious. *Of course,* Nicky thought, *I could be projecting my own feelings onto her. After all, that's how I feel about all of them.*

When they found out the truth, would they turn on her? How could they not? *But does it matter?* Nicky asked herself. *Of course not,* she responded.

But then, Nicky knew she was lying to herself. She wanted to find a home, a place where she was trusted and could trust. Although she had only been in Spring Falls for a short time, she had fallen in love with it. And now, these people who had each other made her want to be part of their lives. Even if she only existed on the outermost parts of their circle, it would be wonderful.

But she had come to destroy their lives, and after she did that, why would they want her?

Only the brief glimmer of hope that they would understand kept her hoping she could stay. She wanted to do the right thing. She thought she was. Perhaps that would save her in the end.

Silently making her way down the steps, head and eyes down as she always did, she heard her name mentioned. She paused and listened and heard something about a house. Was Judith already kicking her out?

But when she saw their smiles, as she walked into the room, she relaxed. A little. And when April asked her if she would like a job helping her with the house she was renovating, Nicky almost cried. She flushed and a small smile sneaked out.

"Is that a yes, Nicky?" April asked.

"I know nothing about designing a house, though." Nicky answered.

"Well, I'll be learning too. But I know I will need help managing all the details. I hope you are good at making order out of disorder."

Nicky paused. Was she? Was that what she had been trying to do all these years? Make sense of the chaos of a missing life?

"I don't know. But yes, I'd like to try."

"Fantastic," Judith said, pushing back her chair. "You two work it out. I have a meeting with Booker later this morning. Nicky, do you want to be there?"

Nicky paused for a moment before saying yes, afraid that Booker and Judith would make her tell what she knew. But she had to be there, because her whole reason for existing all these years was to find Sara, and now she had help.

Her early morning desire to run faded away, replaced by an intense desire to be wanted.

April squinted at Nicky, wondering what she was hiding, and then decided to not think about it.

"I'll change and we'll go," April said.

Nicky nodded, staring at the cinnamon buns.

"Eat them!" Judith said. "There is plenty more where they come from. And April, why not call Marsha and take her along with you? She might like to help too."

"Why didn't I think of that?" April answered, wondering why she hadn't. Marsha needed a push in some direction to get on with her life. Getting Nicky and Marsha to help her would feel fantastic. A group effort was much more fun than doing things alone.

Waving goodbye at Judith, April called Marsha. When a half asleep Marsha answered the phone, April didn't ask. Instead, she said she and Nicky were picking her up in thirty minutes, so get ready. They'd bring coffee. "Wear clothes that can get dirty," she said before hanging up, not caring that Marsha mumbled that she couldn't.

She knew Marsha. She'd be ready. Angry maybe, but ready. *Maybe Marsha could be her renovation project, along with the house.* Then, looking at Nicky, too pale, too thin, looking as if she lived on the streets, she added to herself, *make that three renovation projects.*

It didn't bother her at all that she knew part of why she wanted to help these two women. It would keep her focused on a new life, and not on Ron and whatever he was up to now. Instead, she was gathering a little community of her own, just like her parents had done.

They were always happy. She planned to be much more like them in the future. Starting now.

Thirty One

April pulled into Cindy's driveway half expecting that she would still need to drag Marsha out of bed. Instead, Marsha was sitting on the porch, coffee in hand, waiting.

Nicky got out of the passenger seat and opened the door for Marsha, who smiled at her but shook her head.

"You stay. I might have to lie down."

As Nicky got back in the car, and Marsha dragged herself into the back seat, April wondered how she hadn't noticed how unlike herself Marsha looked. Now she had two women in her car who appeared to be lost in life and wondered if she had gotten herself in over her head.

She had a huge new house to remodel, a new business to start, and two lost women. Was putting all this together a good idea?

Too late now, she said to herself.

A few minutes later she had pulled into the driveway of her house, once again startled at the size. What was Ron thinking?

"Wow," Nicky said, getting out of the car. "This is your house?"

April took a deep breath before answering. "It is, and boy, does it need help. Perhaps you two could help me turn it into something both beautiful and useful? Seth is going to be the foreman, and is helping me with the design, but Janet and Mimi suggested I film it all and start a design business."

"Designing houses?" Marsha asked from the backseat, her legs halfway out of the car.

"I think so. I hope to discover what I want to do while I am doing it. But I also want to turn this home into something useful. It's too big for just two people to live in. I was thinking of living upstairs and having some kind of business downstairs."

"Is it zoned for a business?" Marsha asked.

"Now see, that's the first thing I need to find out. I was hoping you and Nicky could help me. Maybe discover what you want to do in the process."

When neither Marsha nor Nicky said anything, April added, "I don't mean anything negative by that. I just thought the three of us could help each other, and the house would be the catalyst for all of us."

"Are you sure?" Nicky finally asked. "You don't know me, and you have all your friends. Why ask me?"

"No, I don't. And yes, I do. And I promise I will ask them for help, too. But you know, I enjoy doing things with people. I work better in a team. I forgot that until recently. So I am redesigning both the house and myself."

"Okay," Marsha said as she got out of the car and headed to the house. She understood what April meant. And this was a chance to get out of bed, or a reason to get out of bed. Perhaps helping April would help her find her way to what she wanted to do.

Nicky remained standing. She felt torn. April, of all people, was extending an offer. Should she take it? Was it the right thing to do?

When she came to Spring Falls, she hadn't expected to like the women whose lives she was going to tear apart. Especially this one.

But she owed her alliance to Sara first. And this was a chance to learn more.

"Okay," Nicky said. "But I don't enjoy working on teams. I like working alone most of the time."

"I understand that," April answered. "We'll find things to do that you can do by yourself."

Well, I've stepped into it now, April thought as she watched Nicky join Marsha at the front door. She knew she was doing the right thing. So she couldn't figure out why a sense of terror came with it.

Thirty Two

B ree hadn't come to the meeting at Judith's office after all, claiming something had come up. Judith had sighed and decided it was probably better that way, because now she and Booker could concentrate on Nicky.

Nicky had walked to the office, coming from April's house, looking more nervous than ever, if that was possible. It was like looking at a live wire ready to snap.

All Judith could hope was that when it did, it didn't touch any of them. On the other hand, maybe they could diffuse her before that happened.

After the meeting, Judith watched Booker and Nicky leave together. Booker held the door for Nicky, looking back at Judith over Nicky's head with a look that told her he hoped he knew what he was doing.

It was a strange pairing. Booker looked enough like a model that his uniform seemed like a prop, and Nicky, although only a few years older, looked old enough to be his mother.

Stress and secrets can do that to you, Judith thought. *Maybe as we solve this mystery, Nicky will let go of some of that stress.* And maybe

Mimi and Janet could help her remake her look the same way they did with April. That was if it was what Nicky wanted.

All women want that, Judith said to herself. *Even if we don't want to admit it.*

Maybe even she wanted one, too. Not now, perhaps after the holidays. Maybe that was something they could all do, go on a spa retreat together. *Hm...* Judith thought. *Something to think about.* Which would be much more relaxing than worrying about Nicky and her long-lost sister.

Booker had brought little to the meeting. All he had was the name of two girls who had gone missing in Spring Falls during the time frame Nicky mentioned. Before leaving the office, he had put one of his people on doing more research on them and their disappearance. But it had been so long ago he had little hope that they would find anything useful.

At the meeting, he had asked Nicky again to just tell him who he was looking for, but she refused, saying she would not be responsible for accidentally accusing the wrong person.

Neither Booker nor Judith believed her. Not about her desire to be right, but that not only did she know, she was sure. What they didn't know was why she didn't tell them.

When they realized they didn't have much to talk about, Booker suggested Nicky go to Jakestown with him. It was possible there was someone there who would remember something that could help them.

Nicky had snickered. "That was over thirty years ago. They are probably all dead or moved away. The town probably isn't there anymore."

"But it is. And perhaps someone still lives there that remembers."

Judith wondered if Booker might be stretching the truth and only wanted to spend some time alone with Nicky, hoping she'd tell him something by mistake. Or trust him enough to share more.

But he had definitely picked the right thing to say because Nicky had agreed. Not giving her a chance to change her mind, Booker had hustled Nicky out the door, glancing back at Judith with his nod of acknowledgment. Judith knew he'd call if he needed her.

All Judith knew about Jakestown was it was a little over an hour away, and it used to be a small farm town. She hoped Booker found some answers, but once she finished with her clients for the day, she was going to do some research of her own.

Perhaps she'd rope Bruce into helping her. She knew it wouldn't take much. They both enjoyed figuring things out. Besides it would give them another excuse to talk.

As Judith opened her computer to the first client of the day, she smiled to herself. It was going to be a good day. There were things to discover, and many things to fix and put right. Her favorite thing to do.

Thirty Three

"I really don't want to go," Nicky said once they were outside. "I never want to see that town again."

Booker held the truck door open until Nicky stepped inside, realizing that she didn't have a choice. She had decided to tell her story, and now that she did, she had to see it through.

Booker made sure she had on her seatbelt, closed the door, walked around the truck, slid into his seat, and started the engine without saying a word. He was taking his truck, so they would fit in better in the town.

Besides, he loved his truck. He'd had it for years and was almost obsessive about keeping it looking good. But this time of year, you couldn't escape the covering of salt that came up from the roads.

He hoped having Nicky with him, and his old truck, would make him look less like someone in authority.

You can never tell in small towns, Booker thought. He didn't really expect to find any answers in Jakestown, but he wanted time alone with Nicky. She knew the answers she wanted him to find, and it would save a lot of time if she just told him. Then he could check the facts instead of trying to find someone from so many years before.

Booker glanced at Nicky settled in beside him, her hair draped over her face, perhaps thinking it would hide how worried she was. He turned on the windshield wipers to clear a slight sprinkle of snow that had fallen while they were inside Judith's office.

As he drove, Nicky stared out the window. It was a beautiful day. The snow had stopped and a bright sun lit up the clear blue sky. Since Nicky wasn't talking, he tapped on one of his favorite podcasts and sat back to enjoy the ride. Eventually, she would talk to him. He'd give her time.

An hour later, he turned off the podcast as the battered and faded sign announcing that they were entering Jakestown came into view.

"How long since you've been here?" he asked Nicky.

"Too long to count."

"Anywhere you would like to go, or suggest we go?"

"It's your rodeo, you pick."

Booker slowed the truck down and pulled to the side of the road.

"Look, you came to us for help. We could have all just gone on with our lives, happily not knowing a thing about you and your sister. Instead, you showed up, looking like a homeless person, acting all angry and pissed off, determined to upset everyone with your story.

"You're the one with an agenda. If you like, we could turn around. I'll take you back to Judith's house to pick up your stuff, and drop you in a new town where you can pretend to be a nobody. We will all eventually forget you and your sister. We have lives to go back to.

"Or you can talk and we can work this out together. Find your sister, or not. Find the person you believe took her, or not. But it's your choice."

Booker stopped talking, knowing that the silence would have to be filled, but not by him. When Nicky still didn't speak, keeping her head turned away, he started the engine and started to turn the truck back to where they had come from.

"No, wait," Nicky said, her head still turned away.

"I'll tell you what I know. But before that, can we visit my parents' grave?"

"Sure. And let's see if there is any food in this town. I'm hungry."

"Food first?" Nicky asked, letting herself smile as she turned to look at Booker. And for the first time, Booker saw the resemblance to the young woman in the picture with her arm around her younger sister.

He had lied, of course. He would have followed up on her sister's disappearance even if Nicky had left town. Something had happened that was wrong. He couldn't let that go.

But he was grateful that Nicky had said yes. Every time he looked at her, she reminded him of the abandoned dog he had adopted not long ago. He had found her lying by the side of the road, barely breathing, ribs showing through her matted fur, and when she looked up at him with a glimmer of hope in her eyes, he was hooked.

And that's what Nicky had done. Let a little hope shine through her smile.

Dang it, Booker thought. *What have we gotten ourselves into?*

Thirty Four

Nicky gasped in astonishment as they drove down the main street of Jakestown. The diner where they used to eat was still there. She pointed, and Booker pulled over.

As Booker rounded the truck to help her down, she stared at the town she had once loved. Although it had always been old, it had been loved. Now it was ancient and unloved. Many of the stores were empty and looked as if they had been that way for a long time.

The town looked and felt the way she did, Nicky thought. *How could one man have done all this damage?*

Her door opened, and Booker extended a hand to help her down. She thought about refusing, but knowing the distance from the door to the ground, she accepted.

Booker noted to himself that he needed to add running steps to the truck if he was going to be having a passenger other than his dog, Addie, in the future. The thought of Bree in his truck made him smile.

The town didn't make him smile. It was so quiet he wondered if the diner was no longer open, but then he saw two old men sitting outside in chairs. They looked as dusty as the town and were so still at first he wondered if they were real until one nodded to him and glanced at his friend and back to Nicky and Booker. Neither smiled.

Nicky hesitated, and Booker took her hand, hooked it through his arm, and headed to the diner, almost wishing he had on his uniform.

"Boys," he said to the two men as he held open the door to the diner, trying not to show his disgust as one man spit tobacco into a coffee can in response.

At least it's not on the sidewalk, Booker thought to himself.

Inside, the diner looked better than it did outside. The bell over the door gave a faint jingle. A waitress in a faded pink uniform with a white apron that had seen better days glanced their way while pouring coffee for the one man at the diner's counter, missing his cup and spilling on the counter when she saw who was there.

"Geez, Louise," the man said, moving away from the hot coffee and looking at the two strangers at the door.

Booker and Nicky slid into the nearest booth, Nicky keeping her head down, Booker nodding at the waitress and the man at the counter.

"What happened to this town?" he whispered to Nicky.

"You know what happened. My sister went missing. My parents died. Small farmers got bought out. People moved to better places to live."

"Coffee?" They both looked up at the woman in the pink uniform holding a coffee pot.

Booker nodded yes. Nicky kept staring.

"Nicky," the waitress said, putting the pot down.

To Booker's surprise, Nicky burst into tears and let herself be pulled up into a hug by the waitress, who had also burst into tears.

"Patty," Nicky whispered.

"Nicky?" the man at the counter said.

Booker stared as Nicky sobbed into the waitress' shoulder who kept saying, "There, there..."

The man from the counter had moved to the booth saying, "Slide over," to Booker, who obeyed, not knowing what else to do.

Moments later, the waitress released Nicky, turned to the front door, locked it, flipped the sign over to say "closed," and pulled down the blind.

Then she slid into the booth beside Nicky, and keeping one arm around her shoulders, reached across to Booker to shake hands.

"Hey, I'm Patty, and this here is John. You're...?"

"Booker. From Spring Falls."

Patty nodded and turned to Nicky. "Where have you been, girl? And what kind of life have you lived? You look like something the cat dragged in."

To Booker's surprise, Nicky laughed. "I do, don't I. Around. Looking for Sara."

"Honey, Sara's been gone for years."

"Well, she knows that, Patty," John said. "Are you any closer to finding her?"

Nicky shook her head. "No. But Booker here said he'd help me stop the man who took her."

"Honey, you know who it was?"

"I think so. And I think you do too, John."

Turning to Booker, Nicky said, "John is the owner of this diner. He knew all of us. It's where we used to sneak off to when we were supposed to be in school. Patty and me used to come in all the time. There used to be a big jar of pickles on the counter, and John used to get one out whenever he saw us coming."

"We had fun, didn't we?" Patty said. "Who knew I'd end up working here? Well, more than that. I married the owner." She smiled across at John.

Nicky stared at the two of them. "Shut the front door!"

Both of them laughed. "Haven't heard that for a while."

"Congratulations?"

"I'm the lucky man here," John said to Booker. "Had to wait until she grew up and then for her to see me as something other than the owner of the diner."

Booker looked at the man beside him and saw tears in his eyes. For a moment, a missing girl was forgotten.

Nicky smiled at the two of them and then looked at Booker.

"When Sara went missing, John told a story that everyone ignored. But I think he saw the man—the boy—that did something to Sara

"That was so long ago, Nicky. I barely remember it. All I remember is she was laughing with some boy I hadn't seen before. That's all. Don't mean he was the one that took her. Besides, no one ever seen him again."

A long silence filled the room.

"Oh," John said. "Like Sara."

Nicky nodded. "Like Sara."

"And that's who you have been looking for all these years?" Booker asked.

"Yes. Although I figured out who the boy was years ago. Patty, do you remember when there were people in town looking at buying Myer's farm?"

"No."

"I do," John said. "They were here for a week or so. Ate at the diner a few times. Now that you mention it, that boy was with them."

"Yes. That boy was with them. At first, I wasn't sure what had happened. A boy? Did Sara run off with some boy? It was so unlike her, I couldn't believe it.

145

"By the time I figured out who the men were, and then found the boy, he was a grown man, with a family of his own. Respectable. And of course, Sara wasn't with him."

Looking across at Booker, she said, "I know. I should have gotten help. But I didn't think anyone would listen to me.

"And for years, I would just pretend it never happened. Then a few years ago I realized I could die, and never know. So I started the search again. Came back to the same idea that it was the boy. Somehow.

"But I still couldn't prove anything. So I've been watching him. I still can't prove anything. Although I know I am right. Which is why, after all this time, I came to get help."

"If it happened in Jakestown, why did you come to Spring Falls?" Booker asked.

"Because you all know him. And I didn't know what else to do."

Thirty Five

As soon as Nicky said the words, "You all know him," she regretted it. But at the same time, she felt as if someone had lifted a hundred pound weight off of her shoulders.

There was a moment of complete silence before Patty asked, "Who is it? What do you mean? How do we know him?"

When Nicky didn't answer, just kept staring at the table, Booker shook his head and sighed, thinking that Nicky was making it so hard when it could be easy. *Probably not for her, though,* he thought.

"No, she means we know him. In Spring Falls."

Patty's face gave away her relief. There was no way she wanted to live with the guilt of not recognizing someone that could hurt Sara.

Reaching out to hold Nicky's hand, she asked, "Well, who is it then, Nicky?"

For Nicky, it was too much. Patty's hand was old now, but it felt familiar and it took her back to before Sara went missing. She thought of all the times they had held hands as they skipped down the street together, for no reason other than that it was fun. Laughing at nothing. Happy just to be happy.

Would she ever be able to do that again? Laugh and be happy just because. She doubted it. However, as she felt Patty's concern for her and the comfort of having a friend, she almost said the name that had been burned into her brain.

But just in time, she stopped herself. What would happen if she was wrong? Or what would happen if she was right?

So instead she said, "I can't. At least not right now."

Nicky looked up at Booker, expecting to see either disappointment or anger, but his face gave nothing away. Instead, he asked Patty what was good to eat.

"Hungry," he said when everyone looked at him. "And I thought you wanted food, Nicky. Plus, you wanted to go see your parents' grave. Let's do that after we eat."

Patty smiled at Booker. She knew what he was doing. Taking the pressure off. *Smart man,* she thought.

Nicky thought the same thing. She had believed what she said would make him angry, or at least frustrated, but neither seemed to occur.

This is worse, Nicky said to herself. *He's going to wait me out.*

Booker nodded at her, a slight smile tugging at the corner of his mouth as if he could see the thoughts rattling around in her brain. Then, glancing down at the menu Patty had brought them, shut it and asked her what was the best thing they made.

"Best burgers east of the Mississippi and pretty good fries, too. Plus coleslaw."

"I'll take it," Booker said, hoping that Patty wasn't exaggerating too much. He was telling the truth that he was hungry, and a hungry Booker was not a patient man. He had put on a good show, but inside he was frustrated with Nicky. He understood what was happening. But it didn't mean he liked it.

"Nicky?" Patty asked.

Closing her menu, Nicky asked for a grilled cheese sandwich and if they still had the pickles, she'd take one of those.

"Sure do, and it won't take long, will it honey?" she asked directing her question to John, who had moved to the kitchen and was waiting at the window to hear the orders.

"Nope," John answered.

"I'll leave you two to talk, and help John out so we can get the food to you faster."

Getting up, she turned the sign to open and unlocked the door, letting in two men who had been waiting at the door. Without stopping, Patty poured two cups of coffee before the men had time to slide onto the bar stools at the counter.

"Small town," Booker said, sipping his coffee and watching the two men.

"Small then, smaller now."

"What is Myer's farm?"

"Myer's farm?"

"You said people came to town to buy Myer's farm. Did they sell it to them or not?"

"I don't know, really. All I knew was Sara was gone. And if you think going to see the farm will give you answers, it won't."

"Not sure that's true. And if you don't end up telling me who the boy is—was—then you know I am going to ask everyone in town every question I can think of. I doubt you want that, Nicky.

"Take your time today. But think about it. We can stay overnight, and in the morning you will tell me, or I start asking."

Nicky nodded, knowing he would be relentless, which is of course what she wanted in the end.

"Okay. Just let me get through seeing my parents' grave, and tomorrow I'll tell you."

"Fair enough," Booker said as Patty slid his plate in front of him.

For the next fifteen minutes, neither spoke. Booker felt like grunting the burger was so good.

As Patty took away the empty plates, she asked, "Didn't I tell the truth?"

"You did. Tell John he is wasted here in this small town."

Patty smiled. "I will, but he'll say that he knows everyone here, and it's quiet and peaceful, so what else would he want?"

"That's a good point," Booker said, thinking that although Spring Falls was bigger than Jakestown, he loved it there for the same reason.

"I heard you said you were staying in town for the night. You could stay at our place or they still have the old motel just outside of town."

Booker smiled at her. "That is mighty kind of you, Patty, but I think Nicky needs a good night's sleep before we head out tomorrow."

Nicky almost cried. It was such a simple thing. To have someone notice how much she wanted to be alone, to sleep or not sleep. Just to have some private time, before everything changed. She couldn't remember the last time someone thought of how she felt and did something about it.

"Will you stop in for breakfast before you leave?" Patty asked.

Seeing Nicky's hesitation, Patty reached into her pocket and pulled out her order pad. Tearing off a page, she turned it over and wrote a phone number on it and gave it to Nicky. Then, thinking about it, she did the same for Booker.

Hugging Nicky, she whispered, "Keep in touch, please."

Nicky nodded, hiding her tears.

"I will."

"Promise?"

"Promise."

Nicky didn't like making promises she couldn't keep, so she silently made a wish that she could and would. It depended on what they found and how she dealt with it. But at that moment, it felt as if a new life was possible for her, and an old friend could be part of it.

Thirty Six

After Nicky had left to go to her meeting with Judith and Booker, April and Marsha spent the rest of the day at the house measuring things and making notes. They sat in different rooms, paying attention to how they felt, and where the sun lit the room. Without leaves on the trees outside, the rooms in the front of the house were filled with sun, which was good in the winter. And in the summer, they would be shady.

They ordered in Thai food and ate upstairs in what April said could be her dining room. But when Marsha pointed out the obvious that there was no kitchen upstairs, April wondered if she had the plan wrong. Maybe they should split the house in half?

"No," Marsha said. "That feels wrong. This house wants to be open. Do you have enough money to put in a kitchen upstairs? It's just you and Ron. It wouldn't have to be big. Put it over the current kitchen so all the plumbing would be there. But here's the question. Stairs. Are you good with having to climb stairs every day? We aren't getting any younger, you know."

April laughed. "Really? I hadn't noticed."

They both laughed then, thinking of how many times they had seen themselves in a mirror and wondered who that person could be.

"Well, I think I have a few good years to go before stairs defeat me. But I could put in an elevator."

The two of them looked at each other and laughed again, knocking over a carton of rice in the process. Laughing still, they cleaned up the mess together, giggling over the idea that someday they would need an elevator.

"Seriously though," Marsha said. "Why not? It would be easier to take stuff upstairs. You have the money. Why not spend it?"

"You're right. Why not? Ron insisted on buying me this enormous house. I should be able to do whatever I need to do to make it fantastic. He already opened an account in my name and put enough money in it to do whatever I wanted to do with this house.

"But I want the house to be useful. How could it be? What about downstairs? What could we do down there? I could put an office where we run the business, whatever that turns out to be. Despite that, there will be plenty of space."

Marsha wiped up the rest of the rice and packed up the leftovers to take downstairs to the refrigerator to keep for later. She had an idea, a tingle of excitement about what she might do with her life. And the house could be the answer, if April was willing.

As if she could read her mind, April said, "Marsha, what are you doing with the rest of your life? Why not you use this space? It could be something arty. Dance, theater, arts... I don't know. But you do. You could make it into something useful."

Marsha put the food down and hugged her friend.

"Is that a yes?"

Marsha nodded. "I don't know what yet. But yes. As long as you help me and we figure it out together."

"Deal," April said.

For the rest of the afternoon, they talked. Marsha told April how lost she felt, and unsure of herself. April listened, knowing exactly what she meant. Together, they imagined what could happen in the house. How they could both build a new life. They could both see how Bree and Cindy could teach there if they wanted to. And Judith, of course would watch over the business end of it.

"All of us together," April said. "I love it. Perhaps we could name it the Ruby House?"

Marsha agreed. They made plans to invite everyone to the house to plan its new life together. Neither of them mentioned Nicky's quest. Both of them pretending that it had nothing to do with them, although they knew that somehow it did.

That night, April couldn't wait to talk to Ron. She had tried calling him, but it just went to voice mail. *Of course, he is off on one of his business trips again*, April thought.

So she called back and left him as long a message as she could about how happy she was about the house. What she wanted to do with it, and told him thank you for giving it to her, providing a way for her to do whatever she wanted with it.

When the message beeped and stopped her from continuing, April called back and left another message. This time thanking him for being there for her all these years. Told him how much she loved him. How grateful she was for having met him that day in history class.

Later that night, she remembered that she hadn't told him about Nicky. So she called back and left one more message. This time telling him the little she knew about Nicky. Told him Nicky had been looking for her sister Sara for over thirty years, and ended up in Spring Falls, of all places, because she believed that someone who lived in Spring Falls was the reason Sara had gone missing.

"Can you imagine?" April laughed, and then before hanging up, added that he might like to help solve the mystery next time he was in Spring Falls, and she hoped that would be soon.

Later that night, as she was falling asleep in her bed at Judith's, April thought about how much her life had changed in the past year. How much more full it had become now that the Ruby Sisters were back together.

The only fly in the ointment was Nicky and her quest. But since it had nothing to do with her, she would not let it disturb her new life. Instead, she'd help Nicky by having her be a part of the Ruby House, Yes, she liked that name. She and Seth had a meeting scheduled for the next day, to plan out the house, and her new business.

It was going to be beautiful. And one day, the kids would visit and be astonished at what their mother could accomplish. *And Ron will be proud too,* April whispered to herself. She couldn't wait to talk to him.

Ron was busy, and didn't listen to April's message until he was ready, but what he did after that was not what April expected.

Thirty Seven

After calling the owners of her house, Bree felt as if she had shed a hundred pounds. She hadn't noticed that leaving the decision open had been so draining. What had she been afraid of?

She knew she would never leave Spring Falls again, especially since now she had her daughter back. And little Rho. It was a second chance and she would not mess it up this time.

Before Rho was born, Bree had worried. What if the baby looked like her grandfather? That Rho had blond hair and blue eyes like her dad had been a relief. It meant her secret was safe. There was no need to tell Mary about her father. No one needed to know. Ever.

So now she could focus on something else, or someone else. Booker. And Nicky.

Although she had skipped the meeting with Judith, deciding at the last minute she couldn't deal with Booker yet, Judith had called and suggested lunch. And Bree knew that meant she would pry for information. 'Cause that's what Judith did.

It wasn't because Judith was mean. It was because Judith needed to know things. Then she wanted to fix them. So Bree knew Booker would be on the agenda at lunch. It was not something she was looking forward to, but Bree knew that sooner or later they would have the Booker conversation. She might as well get it over with.

And she was ready. Because before she left for lunch, Bree had a private conversation with Paul out in the garden. It was a warm day in December. The kind that rarely came around, but made you hope that perhaps winter wouldn't be that bad. It was never true. But while it was happening, it felt like a blessing. Sitting on the bench in her garden, Bree felt the sun warm on her face and watched little white clouds sail through the crystal blue sky playing peek-a-boo with the open tree branches.

The design of the small garden was clear, even though nothing was blooming. She had spent a few afternoons in the fall trimming everything back to prepare for the return of spring. The last of the fall leaves lay in the garden beds, keeping the plants warm over the winter. Bree knew that just because she couldn't see what was happening, many wonderful things were going on within each plant and tree. They were resting and gathering all that they needed to bloom again in the spring.

Seasons always reminded Bree of how life worked. Life wasn't always in the visible blooming stage. Sometimes it happened out of sight, and in the garden's case, it happened underground. The garden reminded Bree that life was always preparing for the new, and it used the past to fertilize the future. *Nothing ever dies,* is what Bree learned in the garden. It just transforms.

That morning Bree sat in the garden with a cup of coffee and one of Judith's cinnamon buns she had reheated in the microwave, and talked to Paul. She knew Paul wasn't actually present. But sometimes he felt so real it was almost as if he hadn't left. Even if it was just her imagination that Paul was there, Bree told him that although Booker was back in her life, it didn't change anything. She would love him forever.

"You know that, Paul, don't you?" Bree said, her head tipped back to the sky.

When an unseasonably warm breeze enveloped her, Bree imagined it was Paul telling her he understood, which only made her miss him even more.

"If only I could see you one more time, Paul," she whispered.

Enough of this, Bree said to herself, and stood to go back into the house. And then stopped and turned around to watch a bluebird flit by and head up into the Japanese Maple that lived in the garden's corner. Bree knew that sometimes bluebirds stayed over the winter. So the part of her that believed in signs pretended that seeing a bluebird also meant that Paul had stayed, too.

"You have unfinished business," Bree heard Paul say. Because if he was alive, that was exactly what he would have said. She knew she had imagined it. But it was what he would have said.

And Bree knew that if Judith knew what the imaginary Paul said, she would agree. So in a small way, Bree was grateful that there were more pressing mysteries to solve other than who was Mary's father.

So later at lunch, when Judith asked how Bree felt about Booker now, Bree was ready to talk about it because it had nothing to do with her secret.

Later, she would ask herself how she could have been so blind.

Thirty Eight

A fter leaving Ron the slew of messages, April went to bed but barely slept. She faced one way, stared at the wall and rolled to the other wall, punched her pillow to a better shape, lay on her back. Nothing worked.

She alternated between excitement over what she could do in the house, and all the work it would take, and worrying that she might not have the ability to do it. Not only was she going to redo the house, start her own business, but she was going to help Marsha start hers. Or at least provide the place for it. And, of course, try to help Nicky by giving her something to do.

She couldn't wait to talk to Ron about it. But since he hadn't called or texted her back, it had to mean that he was out of town on business. It bothered her. And that it bothered her, bothered her even more. Because she should know better. After all, ever since they moved to Silver Lake, Ron had been going out of town on business.

At first, she hated it. She felt lonely. She had lived within the small community of The Ruby Sisters since first grade, and once they moved, she had no one but Ron. Ron, who was barely home.

She missed having friends. They would argue, but Ron always won. His excuse was he needed total concentration to close the deals he was working on.

"Do you enjoy having enough money to have anything you want?" Ron would ask her, and she always had to admit that she did. So she had learned to not miss him when he was gone, and to be content when he came back. Besides, after the children arrived, they kept her busy.

But when their children moved away, and made lives of their own, with only an occasional phone call to check in, the hole in her life opened again. Only Judith and her weekly calls kept her afloat.

Then when Paul sent a letter to all the Ruby Sisters, asking them to help Bree everything changed. When she had told Ron she was going to Spring Falls to help Bree with the rest of the Ruby Sisters, and he threw everything out of the refrigerator and screamed at her, something inside of her clicked. She wanted a life of her own, and she would make one with or without his help.

April knew that even with that determination, if Judith's voice hadn't guided her home, she probably wouldn't have done anything but clean up and be the dutiful wife again. But she had gathered her courage and returned to Spring Falls. And waited for Ron to apologize and come to her.

Surprising everyone, including her, Ron had done exactly that. And although he never said it, he bought her this enormous house to make up for what he had done. But April knew he was also reminding her that she had all the money she needed because he worked for it, and he needed his freedom to do it.

Although she hadn't wanted the house, now she did. And she wanted to tell him about what she would do with it. And thank him for buying it for her.

But all that will have to wait, April said to herself. *He'll come to see and will be over the moon about her plans.* She was sure of that. He always came back from trips happy. Well, not always.

On those rare occasions he was morose, bitter, and angry, she had learned to be as unobtrusive as possible. His bad mood was because he didn't close the deal, he'd say, and she'd work extra hard at making him his favorite foods and being the wife he wanted her to be.

So she hoped this trip worked out, because she wanted him to be happy about her decisions.

As April rolled over one more time, trying to get back to sleep, she heard Judith in the kitchen, and in a few minutes she smelled coffee and realized there was no point in trying to sleep.

"Morning," April said, slipping into the kitchen. "Is Nicky still sleeping?"

"Booker texted and said the two of them were staying in Jakestown. They'll be back today."

"Why?"

"No idea. Maybe Nicky needed more time there."

April shrugged. "I asked her to help me with the house. I thought it might help her feel more settled."

Judith stared at April over her coffee cup. Something was off. "That's why?"

"Honestly. I don't know. I think so. I think I want to help someone as lost as her. But I think I am afraid of her too. Maybe it's because she's so afraid. And when she looks at me, I see pity in her eyes. Why would that be? What would she feel sorry for me for? And I don't think she wants to feel pity. I think she wants to be mad at me. But for what? I don't know her. She doesn't know me."

Judith waited, wondering if what she was thinking was worth saying out loud. And then remembered that they had promised each other not to keep secrets. Besides, this wasn't really a secret. It was just an idea.

"What if she does know us? Why else did she come to us? I know she believes that what happened to her sister is connected to Spring Falls. So she must believe that we are part of it."

"But why? We never met her sister."

"I know. But maybe someone we know did."

"Like who? Why not go to them instead of us?"

Judith stared at April and wondered if she should say the next thing on her mind, and decided not to. Booker said that Nicky had told him more, but he wanted to check out her story first.

She would keep it to herself, for now anyway. April was as happy as she had ever seen her. Why not let her be that way at least for a little while longer.

So instead of what she was thinking, Judith asked her about the house. When April told her about Marsha's idea, Judith laughed out loud in delight.

"What a great idea! I can't wait to get started."

"Well, we need to meet with Seth. And I forgot, Cindy asked me to stop by the gallery to help them plan their holiday party. Do you want to come with me?"

"Can't. I need to catch up on my business. At the end of the year, everyone starts worrying that they didn't do something right. And sometimes they are right about that and we need to clean it up.

"But I am looking forward to talking to all of you about your and Marsha's new business. Any idea what you'll call it?"

"Too soon, Judith," April laughed. "But we did name the house."

Judith tipped her head, waiting for the answer.

"It's the Ruby House, of course!"

Judith smiled and hugged April. "Of course! Let's celebrate and meet for dinner tonight at ParaTi's. I'll call Bree if you'll ask Marsha and Cindy."

"Just us?" April asked.

"Just us." Judith answered. "I think we just need a Ruby Sister's night out to talk about the Ruby House."

Both of them laughed at the idea of a night out because their version of a night out would be dinner and a lot of giggling. And then they'd all go home to bed. No late partying for them anymore.

Neither of them knew that they would be thinking of that dinner for many years as the dividing line between one life and another, and the chasm they all fell into.

The chasm they had to pull themselves out of in order for each of them to make a new version of life. It would be harder for some than others.

Thirty Nine

As Judith and April were drinking coffee in Judith's kitchen planning their day, Ron was listening to April's messages. Sitting on the bed in the hotel, he glanced in the mirror hanging on the wall and smiled, pleased with himself. He had done the right thing buying her that house. It wasn't surprising. He always did the right thing.

But April thanking him for the house and being so excited about it made him happy. Happiness was an emotion he could feel. There were other emotions he had to learn to portray so people would see him as normal. Normality was something he cultivated.

He'd watch how other people reacted to situations, trying to read their emotions. Then he would see if he could feel the same thing, or at least look as if he felt the same thing.

He enjoyed fitting in. He loved being around people. Probably because he could talk almost everyone into almost anything, and that made him happy. Feeling happy was much easier than feeling frightened or sad. Which wasn't a bad thing. He hoped that people who knew him saw him as a cheerful person. Easy to be around, even if he was very private about his life. And yes, demanding. But

Ron couldn't see how that was a bad thing. It brought order and calmness to situations.

Being calm was easy for him. Except sometimes if something provoked him into reacting against them. But that rarely happened. Staying calm was one reason he made as much money as he did. He didn't react the way everyone else did. And what seemed to frighten other people didn't really frighten him.

After listening to the messages, Ron lay back on the bed, hands folded behind his head, and thought back on his life and how he had learned the skills that had made him so successful.

He had discovered his gift of not reacting as a child. When his father drank, which was almost all the time, he enjoyed creating chaos, which included frightening people, starting with his own family.

His mother would react when his father would walk silently into a room. His father had tried sneaking up on Ron, but it never worked. As much as he tried, his father could never scare him. Which made his father angry. The more passive Ron was, the angrier his father got. Ron thought that not being able to control his son was another reason his father seemed to hate him.

When he got older, his father sometimes made him go with him on his trips. Ron couldn't understand why, since most of the time his father hadn't wanted him around. However, it turned out to be a good thing for Ron, because it was on those trips that he had discovered that he was good at meeting people, especially girls. Which was handy for a teenage boy. *Well, it's handy as an adult, too,* Ron snickered to himself.

Eventually, his father gave up on both him and his mother. He left one day for a trip when Ron was sixteen and never returned, leaving his mother, who had come back, to struggle to raise him with the little money he had left them in the bank. They managed together for a few years and then she got sick and died.

This was not the story he told as he got older. Everyone thought he had a happy home life, and then both parents died when he went to college. It was easier to tell that story, than the one that was true. Besides, he had learned to be a master storyteller.

After his father left, he had done what he could to make his mother happy. He had done it even though she had done nothing for him when his father was around. His goal was to make her happy. If it meant he had to overlook how she treated him in the past, he would do it. To see if he could. For himself. To be happy.

And now he had April to make happy. And like his mother, she had fallen in line with what he wanted.

Satisfied with himself for doing the right thing for April, Ron sat up and opened his small travel suitcase that lay beside him. There was nothing in it that didn't look normal, or that he couldn't replace.

He had learned that lesson well when April had run off to Spring Falls with his suitcase. It was then Ron realized he didn't need most of what he had been bringing on trips with him. And if he needed something, he could always buy it. He was no longer the boy whose father left him and his mother without money. Now, he was a very wealthy man.

Still, he loved both packing and then opening his ordinary, if very expensive, suitcase, because it was the dividing line between being home and being some place else. He didn't travel as his dad had to buy properties from people and change their lives forever. No, he traveled for himself. He was looking for properties, but not the same kind as his father. And he paid nothing for them. But like his father, he changed their lives forever.

In that way, he and his father were the same. And like him, Ron liked to sneak into people's lives, startle them, and create chaos. Like the game of making money, the game was easy for him, and it made him extremely happy. A happiness he could feel deep into his being. It would last for a month, maybe two, and then he'd have to travel again. Find someone new to startle, and change their lives forever.

His father traveled to small towns, but Ron learned early on that he needed to travel to big cities. There were more women. More choices. Fewer chances of being seen. Even with the cameras that seemed to be everywhere, he knew how to not be seen. Or seen, but not recognized.

Yes, Ron said to himself. *I know how to make myself happy. And in a day or so, if all goes well, my happiness levels will soar once again, and I'll go home to April, my perfect wife.*

That Ron rarely thought about his children didn't seem strange to him. They had their lives. He had his. At least he wasn't an abusive drunk like his dad, and didn't walk out on them. His children were used to him not being there all the time. He had trained his family well.

Listening once again to April and her excited message, Ron smiled. It was going to be the perfect day. His wife was happy. He was in a new city. Life was full of possibilities.

Checking his new look for this trip in the mirror, he gave himself a thumbs up and headed out to have breakfast at the small diner he had seen down the street. It was a good place to look for a new piece of property.

Forty

B efore going into the office, Judith called Bruce. *This early morning call thing to Bruce is getting to be a habit,* Judith thought.

When she stopped to think about it—which she tried not to do too often—she wondered how Bruce had become the person she always called when she wanted to think something through.

Maybe because he loved to solve problems the same way she did. Well, not exactly the same way. She wanted to find out about things so she could fix any problems she found. He wanted to search out answers to questions he had, or discover new questions and find the answers to them. It was the same, but different. There were many things like that about the two of them. They did things differently, but with the same outcome in mind.

First Judith texted Bruce to see if he was up for a call, and within seconds he had responded "Yes!"

Putting her headset on so she could talk while she got ready to leave, Judith waved goodbye to April and called. As always, his voice made her feel both excited and calm. Which didn't seem possible, but there it was.

As they said "hi" to each other, Judith stood at the front window and watched April turn the corner heading to the gallery to help with the holiday design, and smiled thinking how wonderful it was to see April so excited about her new project.

"What's up?" Bruce asked.

"I have an idea, and wanted to run it by you."

"I'm listening."

Judith paused, and then after filling him in with the latest about Nicky and Booker, she said, "I know Nicky believes Sara is dead, but what if she isn't?"

"Okay. Oh. You want to go looking for her, don't you?"

"Yes!" Judith said, bouncing on her toes. Something her friends knew she did when she got really excited about something.

Plopping onto the couch, Judith said, "Why not? Everyone else is focused on who this guy is that Nicky believes took her, but why don't we focus on looking for Sara? Maybe she isn't alive, and Nicky is right, but finding what happened to her would give her closure."

"But if they find the guy, won't he tell?" Bruce asked, playing the devil's advocate, knowing that was exactly what Judith wanted him to do.

"Maybe. Maybe not. Even so, wouldn't it be fun? Working together. You know…"

Bruce knew. More than once, the two of them had talked about him moving to Spring Falls and working together somehow. They rarely said to live together. At the moment, they were only great friends, and now they could be partners searching for Sara.

However, without mentioning it to Judith, Bruce had talked to his friend, another estate planning attorney in town, about buying his business. His friend was interested and the two of them were slowly working out what that would look like.

He had also talked to a real estate agent about selling his home. All of which he was doing without telling Judith because he didn't want to scare her off. But he knew it was nearing the time when he had to tell her, or just call all of it off.

Of course, he could still sell the business and move somewhere else, but Bruce knew what he wanted was to live in the same town as Judith.

In the back of his mind, Bruce wondered if Paul had been psychic. Had he seen the future where all the Ruby Sisters came together, and Bree found her daughter, and most of all that the attorney he hired to handle his last wishes would fall for the beautiful redhead named Judith?

"Bruce?" Judith said, breaking him out of his daydream.

"Yes, lets."

"Together?"

"Absolutely. Where do you want to start? What would you like me to do?"

Judith paused, afraid to ask.

"You want me to come there?"

Judith wanted to yell "yes" into the phone, but calmly said instead, "Would you?"

"I'll cancel my appointments and be there tomorrow morning."

Judith smiled, and bounced on the couch, happy he couldn't see her.

"You can stay at my house. It's already full of guests, and that way we can talk whenever we want to. I'll make some phone calls in the meantime."

Bruce had always stayed at a motel in town, so it took him a moment to realize what she had said.

"You're sure you want me there?"

"Well, it will be different. A man in the house. But maybe Nicky will talk to you, and you know April loves you."

There was a long pause as both of them thought about what she had just said, both of them adding in their heads, *and I love you too*, but not willing to admit it or say it out loud.

"See you in the morning, Judith," Bruce said, hung up, and then started making calls. The first one was to his friend. It was time to turn his business over to him. Then a call to his real estate agent saying he was ready. She could put his house on the market.

Bruce knew it was a crazy move. But he also knew that he wanted to be near Judith, even if all they ever were to each other were best friends. Tipping back in his chair, he stared out at the apple tree outside his window.

Leafless now, its delicate structure of limbs and twigs stood out against the clear blue sky like a patchwork of intricate lace. The tree, like him, was preparing for a new season. He'd miss the tree. He'd miss his clients and his business, and even his home. But a new life was calling, and he was going to answer this call.

After Judith hung up, she wondered if Bruce had heard the underlying message in her call, surprised that it was there. Something she'd have to deal with later. Right now, she wanted to find Sara. Dead or alive.

It was the dead part that reminded her of what Grace Strong had mentioned in passing when she had helped them find answers to Paul's past. She had said she had friends who could see the people who lived in the in-between. What if that was where Sara was?

Grace and Judith had talked a few times since Grace had returned to Doveland. Judith had thought it only polite to fill her in when Bree found her daughter, and after Rho's birth. Now perhaps Grace could help them out again and send her friends to Spring Falls. It was a shot in the dark, but worth a try.

And she would call her computer friend that no one knew except her. Matt was a mystery. All she knew about him was that if she paid him well, he found answers. For all she knew, his name wasn't Matt.

First call Grace, then Matt, then Bree to tell her about the dinner that night. Then to the office, Judith thought as she bounced off the couch, feeling as if she could conquer the world. *It was going to be a great day!*

Forty One

B ooker had asked for two adjoining rooms in a motel that looked as if it had gotten stuck in the 1970s. But it was clean and warm, as long as you didn't mind the rattle of the radiator as the heat poured through it. Booker kicked it a few times to make it stop. It didn't work.

Nicky poked her head around the open door between the rooms and said, "You know, everyone kicking it is probably why it makes that noise in the first place."

"You're probably right. Hey, if you're hungry, we could order pizza. Is there a place that delivers?"

"You think I would know?"

The two of them had done what Nicky wanted, visited her parents' grave. They rested under a large red maple in a small graveyard beside an old stone church. Booker had waited in the car. He could see her in the distance—sometimes standing and pacing. Sometimes sitting and staring up at the tree. And then, bent over head to the ground.

He had almost gone to check on her, but then a squirrel startled her and she sat up. Booker hoped she was done then, but it seemed she had just begun. Sitting up she started waving her gloved hands around as if she was having a conversation and he figured she might just be getting started saying what she wanted to say to her parents.

Although he had dressed for the cold, he was tired of starting and stopping the car to heat it up, so he walked to the church, hoping it would be open and warm.

It was both. Sighing in relief, he took in his surroundings. Is the whole town stuck in the 70s? Booker wondered. Could the disappearance of one girl have kept an entire town from moving on?

As if in answer to his question, a tall, slender man dressed in black with a white collar tucked inside his shirt opened the door at the front of the church and headed his way. Booker thought he was probably in his seventies, but then who could tell these days?

"Reverend?"

"Or Tom, take your pick. Actually, prefer Tom."

"Booker. Sorry, waiting for a friend and I was getting cold so I came inside."

"Happy to give you a place to wait. Is there anything you need that I could help with? Maybe a little spiritual guidance?"

Booker laughed. "I probably need more than a little. But perhaps you could give me insight into the town."

"I assume you actually have a period of time in mind? Would you mind if we sit? Sometimes my back bothers me if I stand too long."

The two of them slid into a pew as Booker asked, "Were you here in 1985?"

Tom looked away and when he turned back, Booker could see unshed tears making his deep brown eyes glitter.

"Ah. I wondered if that was her in the graveyard. So Nicky finally came back. It was a terrible thing. Her sister went missing. Her parents grieved. Nicky got angry. Her parents died. The town gave up."

"Just because a girl went missing?"

"I know it doesn't sound as if that would do it. But we were a small town. We all knew each other. We all knew Sara. A beautiful girl. Kind, generous, always smiling. We loved Nicky, too, but Sara was the golden girl. Like an angel, really. Maybe she was too naïve for this world.

"We all knew something terrible had happened. And we didn't know if one of us had done it. That's really what tore the town apart. We separated from each other. Suspicion. Fear."

"John at the Diner said he thought it was because of the boy she was seen with. He was with the men who wanted to buy Myers Farm?"

"Ah, that." Tom took a song book out of the back of the pew and opened it at random, read a few words and shut it again.

"I always find comfort from music and the word of the Lord. I highly recommend it."

Booker smiled. "I'll give it a try. What about the boy and the farm? Do you think they had something to do with her disappearance?"

"It's possible. That definitely changed the town. When they bought Myers farm it was the final push that ruined the town. The man promised the world to the town, but his company never did any of it. The man and the boy left town. And the corporation he represented did only enough to get government subsidies for not planting crops. If you can believe the injustice of that.

"Sometimes I do believe in evil, you know. I pray to remind myself that good is more powerful. But that corporation was and is evil. And perhaps the man and boy that came with them were too."

"Is it possible that you remember the name of the man who was here?"

"Not his first name. Just the last. Page. His last name was Page."

Before Booker could ask more, Nicky had stuck her head in the door and seeing Tom, whispered, "Reverend?"

After a long hug and a few whispered words, Tom let Nicky go and turned to Booker. "I wish you both the best of luck. It's time this town had some closure. Perhaps if we knew what happened, we could start again."

Turning again to Nicky, still holding her hands, he added, "Nicky, love, no matter what, it's time to start living again. Even if you don't find her or what happened, please don't let the rest of your life slip away. And come visit this old man again, please."

Nicky nodded, tears overflowing.

As they walked to the truck, Booker said, "The people of this town loved you, didn't they?"

Nicky stopped and looked back at the church, Tom standing in the doorway waving.

"I didn't know that. I thought they only loved Sara."

As Booker helped her up into the truck, he thought about what Tom had said to Nicky about not letting the rest of her life slip away. It sounded to him like it was directed at him, too. Perhaps the Reverend saw through him and recognized how he was just marking time.

Now in the motel room with the banging heater, a woman who looked marginally better after a day of realizing that people cared about her, Booker decided to talk to Bree after this was all over. Who knew where that would lead? Maybe nowhere. But it was time to stop hiding from what happened all those years before.

Like Nicky, it was time to let go of the past. And to do that, they needed to find out what happened. He hadn't told her that Tom knew the name of the man who had come to town.

He hadn't told her because he didn't want it to be true. Perhaps it was a different man and boy with the last name of Page. But something told him it wasn't. But he could wait until morning to find out.

Right now, he wanted pizza and a good night's sleep. In the morning, he'd call the office and have them check on the timing and the people. There was no way he was going to ruin someone's life on speculation.

Perhaps that's why Nicky is afraid to say it, he thought. He was too.

"What about pizza, sleep, maybe breakfast at the diner and then we'll head back to Spring Falls?" Booker asked Nicky.

She knew what he was really saying. It was time. And she was ready.

"Yes, first pizza, then sleep, the diner, and then back to Spring Falls."

Forty Two

April had spent the day doing what she had finally discovered she loved to do. Design things. Specifically rooms and buildings and maybe even what went in them. In high school, she and Cindy had taken art classes together, but that was because Cindy always loved art and April loved being with Cindy.

But art hadn't clicked for her the way it had for Cindy. She would have never dreamed the two of them would do art again together. Not in the same way, though. She wasn't picking up a paintbrush. She was making spaces for experiences.

And April wondered why Cindy wasn't doing art herself anymore, at least not the way she used to. But she didn't ask. Maybe Cindy was painting and wanted to keep it to herself.

Spending the morning with Cindy at her art gallery preparing for the open house had been fun and fulfilling. The gallery was already beautiful with the art and the lights, but she added a few extra details, which Cindy, Mimi, and Janet said made it perfect. The four of them had laughed and giggled, and while they worked, she had come up with more ideas for her house.

After lunch, she met Seth and Marsha at the house and they had planned, schemed, designed, and dreamed. The afternoon had flown by in a haze of excitement. Nicky hadn't returned from Jakestown, so Seth was the one who found out that she could have a business in the house as long as they provided enough parking. So they spent part of the day planning where they could put it. April didn't want it to be an eyesore, but it had to be easy to get into and out of.

"I think we are going to need a landscaper to help with this," Seth had said, and promised to find them one after doing a bit of research himself.

When April mentioned they were having a Ruby Sister's dinner at ParaTi's, Seth said he knew about it. He was on babysitting duty because Mary had switched shifts so she could be their waitress for the evening. So later, when April walked in the door at ParaTi's, it didn't surprise her to see Mary hovering over Bree and Judith, who had arrived before she did.

Marsha and Cindy came in the door behind her, and the three of them took in the scene. Mary had her hand on her mother's shoulder and Bree was smiling as if she was the luckiest woman in the world. Judith motioned them over, and Mary looked up and waved.

"Who would have thought we'd have this again?" April said to Marsha as they made their way to the table.

"Even better than before," Marsha said, and Cindy nodded in agreement.

Dinner was just what Judith had hoped it would be. Bree shared some of her ideas for her new book. Cindy talked about the gallery and what April had done to make the holiday open house spectacular. Marsha expanded the basic idea of what she was going to do in the downstairs of April's house and asked for help in designing what that would become.

BECA LEWIS

Judith shared that Bruce was coming to town the next day, which made everyone look at her in anticipation. She knew what they wanted to know. Were she and Bruce an item? It was Cindy who helped her out.

"We already know that you two are involved, so you can stop pretending. It's a good thing, Judith."

"Yes, it is!" Everyone agreed.

"Yes, what is?' Mary asked as she delivered the desserts. They always ordered a few different ones and then rotated them around the table so everyone could share.

It was the Ruby Sister way, Mary thought.

"That Judith and Bruce are an item," Bree said, smiling up at her daughter.

"Oh, I agree! He seems like a wonderful man. Besides, wasn't he the key to bringing us all together? I mean, Paul was, but didn't he pick Bruce for a reason? Or at least that's what it seems to me."

"Here, here," all the women said, lifting their water glasses and clinking them together. "To Bruce and Judith!"

Judith blushed, her face almost as red as her hair, but her smile gave her away.

"Thanks, Mary," she whispered as Mary refilled her coffee cup.

Mary smiled at the group. In a million years, she would have never thought that she could have this many mothers, this many women who cared about her. They were her family.

And of course there was Seth and now Bruce. Two men of integrity and kindness. She didn't include Ron, only because she didn't know him. Perhaps he would make the list later.

April thought it was the perfect ending to a perfect day. And then Booker and Nicky walked in the door.

Forty Three

B ree saw them first, and little tingles ran up her arm and neck when Booker glanced her way. The reaction surprised and annoyed her. Even though she knew Paul wanted her to move on, in truth, she didn't want to. Life was good the way it was.

But seeing the look on Booker's face, and the different way Nicky was carrying herself, changed the tingles from pleasure to fear.

They must have found something, Bree thought.

It was exactly what Judith thought, too, seeing the two of them. They weren't happy. They were worried. For a moment Judith felt as if a dark pit had opened up beneath the table, and they were all plunging down into it.

Then Booker smiled, and Nicky attempted to, and the feeling vanished, making Judith wonder if she had imagined it. But when Bree glanced over at her, looking worried, she knew she hadn't.

"You're back," Cindy said, as the two approached the table. "Join us. Did you eat? Do you want coffee, dessert?"

"No. Sorry, can't stay," Booker said, responding to Cindy but looking at Bree. "I thought you all might be here when no one was at the house, Judith. So I brought Nicky to you. I'm heading home. Perhaps in the morning you and Nicky could come by the station?"

Marsha squinted up at Booker, wondering what he wasn't telling them. Nicky looked better, but she was wound up, like a jack-in-the-box waiting to pop.

"Nicky, sit, have a bite of dessert," Judith said, standing. "Let me walk you to the door, Booker."

He nodded, trying not to look at Bree again.

When they were far enough from the table, Judith said, "You know something, don't you?"

"Not something I want to talk about right now. Bring Nicky to the station in the morning and I'll tell you what I know so far."

"Why don't you tell us all?"

"Judith, what I think I know will break one of your friend's hearts. There is no way I am going to talk about this to anyone else until I am sure enough that it has to be said."

"Did Nicky tell you?" Judith asked, grabbing his arm.

"Look. That's it for tonight. Go back to the table. Don't alarm everyone acting like a raging Viking. Smile. Be nice. Let it go. Let them all have one more night before we throw everything they know up in the air."

"If you're right."

"If I'm right."

Judith did exactly what Booker asked. She smiled, patted him on the shoulder and returned to the table, asking for more coffee from Mary, as she pulled up a chair.

"What was that all about?" Marsha whispered.

"Nothing important," Judith answered.

April had watched the scene play out and felt as if a hurricane had whipped through her insides and blown everything around. There was no logical reason to feel that way. But she did.

The moment she had seen Booker and Nicky walk in the door, the ground had started trembling. Judith's calm manner and smiles didn't seem normal. Nicky was actively trying not to look at her. Something was definitively wrong.

"I'm coming to the station with you tomorrow," April said.

Marsha looked around the table. "We all are. I think Booker might have forgotten that we Ruby Sisters stick together. We know something is going on and we are going to find it out together."

As Nicky trembled by her side, Judith nodded. "Agreed. Together."

Once again, glasses were raised and clinked together as they said, "Here, here!"

Turning to Nicky, Judith added, "It's better this way, Nicky. You'll see."

All Nicky could do was nod. She wondered if, after all the story was told, the group would still accept her. She would understand if they didn't. She hadn't fit in anywhere for so long, it would just be one more time that she was an outsider.

There was no way she was going to hope that anything would be different from what it had always been. And nothing would bring Sara back now, anyway. And those two things were all she had ever truly wanted. Sara in her life, and someone who cared about her.

That would not happen now.

Judith texted Booker that they would be at the station at eight. He better be ready. She didn't tell him that everyone was coming. He couldn't stop them, anyway. For better or worse, they would hear the story, and decide together what to do about what they heard.

And even though she had just met Nicky, she would protect her. Nicky had come to her asking for help. And no matter what Nicky had been hiding, it hadn't been something she had done. It was what she knew.

Knowing that Bruce would be there in the morning helped calm Judith down. Maybe Matt, doing his magic with the computer and internet, would have found something about Sara by morning, too. Either way, at least they were doing something.

Judith debated telling Nicky what she and Bruce were doing and decided not to. She didn't want to get her hopes up until they knew more. And depending on the news in the morning, it might be just the thing that broke her, and Judith wasn't sure if even she could fix her after that.

Forty Four

J udith woke early as usual and made her way downstairs as silently as possible. She had two guests in her home, and soon she'd have a third one. This was not something she ever thought would happen. A full house.

She had inherited the house from her parents and had lived in it since she was six. She was grateful because she had always loved it, although as an only child she had often wished for more people in the house than just her and her parents. Now she had her wish. Not siblings, but friends.

Probably better that I didn't have siblings given how I am, she thought to herself. *I would have tried to run their lives.*

It surprised Judith that she thought of Nicky as a friend. She barely spoke. She had arrived, angry and withdrawn. And she had a terrible secret that Judith knew in her bones would change everyone's lives.

But she was ready for it. And she would battle it and bring it to a peaceful resolution, no matter what it was. Besides, Nicky needed a friend. She and the Ruby Sisters could do that for her. But what would be the best would be to find out what happened to Sara. That was a gift she and Bruce might be able to give her.

Judith doubted that either April or Nicky were asleep, but she didn't want to be the reason they got out of bed this early, so she quietly made coffee and went into her office and shut the door.

The room used to be her parents' master bedroom with its own bathroom, making for the perfect quiet retreat when there were guests in the house.

The first thing she did was check her messages to see if Matt had found anything. Disappointed that there was nothing, she thought about asking him again but decided against it. It wasn't the hour, Matt didn't keep hours, it was because Judith knew Matt hated being micro-managed.

Restless, needing to do something, she decided to call Grace Strong about her friends that saw people into the in-between. Grace had mentioned them when they had met her while following the instructions in Paul's letter to Bree.

Judith had filed the information away as a curiosity, thinking that wasn't possible. But Grace was sure that's what they did, and if Sara was dead, perhaps they could find her that way. Although she didn't understand how that worked, it was worth a try. She didn't understand how many things worked, but that didn't mean she wouldn't use them.

She knew Grace was an early riser, so she wasn't worried that she would wake her up, but she texted first to make sure she was up for a phone call. Thirty minutes later, Grace had confirmed that her friends Bryan Anderson and Rachel Windsor would be glad to help and would be in Spring Falls in a few days. They'd call her before they got there and arrange a meeting.

After thanking Grace and hanging up, Judith shook her head at what she had done. It was crazy enough that she decided not to tell anyone, except maybe Bruce. It was a long shot, after all. Besides, even if it were possible to see someone who had died, she didn't really want Sara to be dead.

Judith heard the shower running and knew at least one of her house guests was awake. The day had begun. A day that Judith knew in her bones would change their lives.

It's an upheaval day, Judith thought. A day that would throw everything up in the air to be rearranged in a new pattern of life. Not that she wanted it to happen, but she couldn't stop what was inevitable. Judith knew she could handle the fallout. She hoped her friends could, too.

Ron almost answered April's fifth call. She never called late at night. Perhaps there was an emergency? He kept waiting for a voice message to find out what was happening, but she just called and hung up repeatedly.

Finally, when he didn't answer the fifth call—he didn't want to set a precedent that he was available while he was away—April left a message.

It wasn't what she said that made Ron's blood run cold. It was how she said it, because all she said was to call her. Nothing about the kids. Nothing about an emergency. Nothing about being excited about the house. Just call her.

Of course, it could mean nothing, Ron thought. But that's not what it felt like.

All he could hear in his head was a voice that kept saying, "Run."

It was completely illogical. Run why? Run where? He had a project to finish. No one knew where he was or what he was doing. Why would he run?

And no, he would not call April back. She knew he was traveling, which meant he was unreachable.

His mind made up, Ron went back to sleep. But in his sleep, he still heard the word. Run.

Forty Five

B ooker had barely slept again, and he felt ragged and uneasy. His back hurt from too much sitting and trying to sleep with a dog in his bed. His neighbor had taken great care of Addie while he was gone, but she had insisted on sleeping beside him, something he usually discouraged, which didn't help.

He wasn't sure if she wanted comfort or knew that he did. Probably both, which is why she also insisted on coming to work with him and was now standing by his side as he waited for Nicky and Judith. At least he had showered and shaved and had on clean clothes. He didn't look or feel great, but it was as good as it was going to get.

It had been a foggy morning, and the clouds were dark and ominous, so he had forgone his daily run. But now, as he stood at the window looking out at the parking lot, he thought maybe he should have run off some of his nervous energy.

Yesterday, after he and Nicky had come back from Jakestown, he had researched what Nicky told him and what he had learned from the Reverend Tom. Called in a few favors, and confirmed what he had heard and what Nicky had known all along. He hated what he had found. He hated that Sara's disappearance involved Bree and her friends. But it did, and he had to tell them.

He had followed all the rules. Did the research. Everything was in order. Now the messy part.

He watched as Judith pulled into the lot with Nicky and April. But then Bree arrived with Cindy. *Crap,* he thought. They all came. But then he realized that, of course they would, and it was probably better this way, anyway.

Another car pulled into the lot, and a man got out he had never seen before. Judith hugged him, and all of them turned and headed towards the station.

Turning to his assistant, he said, "We're going to need more chairs."

A few minutes later, everyone was in his office, chairs circling his desk. Booker wasn't sure if he felt trapped or safe. Probably both. Trapped in the telling, but safe knowing these were people who would protect one another. He hoped they didn't hate the messengers, both him and Nicky. He could handle it, though he wasn't sure Nicky could.

As they settled in, Judith introduced the man as Bruce Dawson, Paul's estate attorney who had helped them carry out Paul's last wishes. Bruce lived a few hours away, and since he was already planning to visit, she had asked him to meet her at the station.

"Early riser?" Booker asked.

"Sometimes. But today, yes. This meeting sounded important, and I wanted to be here to help."

"Well. This is not a meeting I wanted to have. But you all deserve to know what Nicky has shared with me and what I have confirmed, because it affects all of you.

"As you know, Nicky came to Spring Falls because she believed that the man responsible for her sister's disappearance, has lived in this town. She also believed that the same man is responsible for multiple disappearances of young women for over thirty years. She figured this out on her own, moving around, asking questions. A lot of research went into her conclusion. However, as you know, she was still reluctant to tell me what she knew, because she was afraid of being wrong.

"Speaking to some residents in Jakestown confirmed that there was a man and his son who were passing through at the time of Sara's disappearance. And it was after learning their name that Nicky finally told me it was the man she had tracked.

"I have set in motion a nationwide search to confirm what she told me, and what I learned in Jakestown. That said, let me assure you, that at this point, although the evidence is primarily circumstantial, the facts are compelling enough to bring you all in and let you know what we have found."

"Because we know this person?" Judith asked.

Booker nodded.

"What do you think this person did?"

"Since we have yet to find any of his victims, we are not sure. All we have found is a pattern. Whenever this man has been in town, a woman goes missing. For years. As I said, it's just a pattern we are following. No other solid proof at this moment."

"You said a man and his son were in Jakestown when Sara went missing. Are you talking about the man or his son?" Judith asked.

Nicky just dropped her head. So it was Booker who answered the question.

"The son. At the time, he was only fifteen."

No one spoke. It was so quiet Judith thought she could hear the tick of the clock in the other room. Beside her she could feel Bruce's fear. It was the same thing she felt.

Years before, she had been in California when an earthquake hit. That was scary enough. But then minutes later she could hear the aftershock coming, rumbling like ground thunder, as it moved towards them. That was terrifying, knowing what was coming.

That's what it felt like now. She could hear the rumble of the words that Booker was going to say. Would those words bring down their world?

Judith turned to look at her friends. They looked as stunned, worried, and frightened as she felt. But it was April who was pale and visibly shaking.

"Are you alright?" Judith asked.

"Don't feel well," April said.

"Bathroom?" Cindy asked.

"Hall, to the right," Booker said.

April shook her head as everyone got up to go with her. "Just Cindy," she mumbled and hurried out of the room, Cindy's arm around her.

Nicky stood up too, looking as if she wanted to run out of the room. Marsha reached up and pulled her gently back to her seat.

"Whatever this is, it not's your fault," she whispered to Nicky. Nicky shuddered and dropped her head again. Perhaps that was true, but if she would have just left it alone, it would have hurt none of these people who she wanted to be her friends.

A long moment passed before Bree asked what everyone was thinking. "It's Ron, isn't it?"

Forty Six

Mimi was in the office taking care of online orders while Janet prowled the gallery making sure everything was in place. She had tipped the spikes of her blond hair with green in honor of the holiday and she wore a tunic that sparkled.

Janet didn't need a reason to wear sparkles, but she loved the holiday season when she wasn't the only one wearing them. She loved the lights, the smells, and even the cold. She wished that the holiday season would go on all winter. But she supposed it made it special that it lasted for such a short time.

Straightening a picture that was a hair crooked, she asked herself what was bothering her. Because something was. Not having Cindy in the gallery in the morning wasn't unusual. Cindy often had business to attend to and meetings to go to, but Janet was worried anyway. Something was off. She just didn't know what it was.

The bell chimed as the gallery door opened and Mary came in, carrying what could only be a baby but looked like a rolled up bag of pink quilting.

"I hope you don't mind me dropping in," Mary said as Janet reached for the bundle and started cooing at the tiny face with bright blue eyes peeking up at her.

"Look Mimi," Janet said, rushing into the office, leaving Mary laughing at the door as she hung up her coat. She was getting used to Rho stealing the show everywhere she went.

By the time she got to the office, Mimi had taken off the bundling and was admiring the onesie Rho had on that was covered with pictures of building tools.

"I assume her father gave her this one?" Mimi laughed.

"Yep," Mary answered. "Said he was putting her to work as soon as she can pick up a hammer."

Rho burped in response, and everyone laughed. "Wearing pink and carrying tools. It's how it should be," Janet agreed.

"Where's Cindy?" Mary asked, picking up Mittens who had wandered into the office looking for the source of all the noise. Mittens peered over at the baby in disinterest and curled up in Mary's lap after first licking her front white paws and kneading a nest for herself.

"Some kind of meeting," Mimi answered.

"But it feels like it's more than that," Janet said.

"What does it feel like?" Mary asked.

"Foreboding? I know that's weird. There's no reason to think that."

Then Rho gurgled and all three women moved in to talk to her, imagining that Rho was telling them a story.

An hour later, Mary got a text from Seth saying a winter storm was moving in. She shared the news with Janet and Mimi and said she had to go. A few minutes later, Rho was a pink bundle again and covered with kisses as Mary shrugged on her coat.

As she and Rho passed the gallery windows, they smiled and waved. Mittens curled around Mimi's feet and she lifted her as they waved back.

"Do you think it's the weather that gave you that feeling, Janet?"

"Could be," Janet said, and added, "But it seems more than that. I know Bree is Mary's mother, but why won't Bree tell her who her father is? I asked her once, and she said it wasn't important. But obviously it is, or why not tell?

"And every once in a while, I see Mary and she does something that reminds me of someone. But I don't know who."

Mimi put an arm around her wife, and the two of them stood in that gallery together as a few snowflakes drifted past the window.

"Sometimes people need to keep secrets," she said, resting her head on top of Janet's.

"I suppose," Janet sighed. "But this one doesn't seem like a good one to keep. Besides, too often secrets end up getting out and hurting people. Seems like it would be better to just say it and get it over with."

Although she didn't say so out loud, Mimi agreed. And she hoped whatever secret Bree was keeping about Mary's father didn't hurt their friends when she found out, because she was sure that one day she would.

Forty Seven

J udith's question covered the room like a black cloud. But
before Booker could answer, his assistant rushed into the room.
"Sorry, but I thought you should know. There has been a
weather alert. A massive winter storm is moving in. Maybe two feet
of snow by tonight."

As if to emphasize her point, there was a crack of lightning
followed by a rumble of thunder.

"A thunderstorm," Booker said. Winter thunderstorms were
rare, but when they happened, they were often more dangerous
than a regular snowstorm, and with a storm moving that quickly,
the situation could turn into a nightmare. It also meant that
because of the early fog making wet roads, they could quickly turn
into sheets of ice.

"Call everyone into the station. We are going to need all hands
on deck."

Booker's assistant nodded and hurried out of the room to make
the calls.

After she left, Booker sighed before answering.

"Yes, Bree. We believe it's Ron, but as I said, there is no actual proof. All we have right now is that Sara was seen with him the day she went missing, Nicky's search for missing women, and the data we have gathered in the last few days from around the country.

"As far as I can tell, there are no missing women from Spring Falls, which could mean it's not Ron. Or it could mean he knows enough to not work where he lives. Or we don't know about them.

"With the community college in town, it's harder to track this metric. But at this point, we don't think anyone is missing.

"However, we are going to have to leave it like this for now. This storm is going to take all our attention. I suggest you all go home and get ready for the storm yourself. Take care of April. I think she suspects that it's Ron. We'll question her and the rest of you after this storm is over."

Giving Bree one last look, Booker left the room and they could hear him giving orders to prepare for the storm.

No one moved. April and Cindy had not returned from the restroom. Everyone else looked stunned. Nicky kept her head down.

Bruce and Judith stood up and Judith said, "Let's go. We can talk about this back at the house. I suggest we go to my house together. If we have to stay in for a few days, I have plenty of extra places for people to sleep.

"Bree, could you get Cindy and April and bring them to my house? Marsha, you and Nicky ride with Bruce. I'll be right behind you. I am going to check on a few things first."

Bree nodded and did what she was told. But part of her had detached itself from her body and she felt as if she was floating above herself, watching what was happening.

Even as she went to get Cindy and April, she did it from a faraway place. Everything that was in place in her life just a few hours before was falling apart.

197

She found the two of them in the bathroom. Cindy was patting April's face with a wet paper towel. Seeing Bree's face, Cindy paled. Whatever had happened since they left the room was bad.

"What's happening?" Cindy asked.

"A weather front is moving in quickly. We are all going to Judith's. She wants you and April to come with me. Marsha and Nicky are going with Bruce."

Cindy didn't need to ask what Judith was doing. She knew she would be trying to fix something. Maybe find out more. Maybe get food. Who knew? But they wouldn't be able to change her mind. It was better to do what she asked.

April hadn't moved. Just stood in front of the mirror staring at herself with red-rimmed eyes. She knew what had happened. She could feel her whole life unraveling one thread at a time. A life she had built up over the years, and only yesterday was excited about adding to it.

April didn't have to be in the room to have heard what they said. Something inside of her woke up the minute they had walked into the station. They had to be talking about Ron.

She shook her head at her reflection. But it couldn't be true. He was her husband. She wouldn't let it be true. She took out her phone and called him, hands shaking so hard she had trouble holding the phone, so she put it down, not caring that the counter was wet. Bree and Cindy watched, knowing what she was doing.

The phone rang and rang and then went to voice mail just as it had done for the last few days. *He's working*, April said to herself. *When he is done, he'll call me.*

Looking up at Cindy and Bree watching her, she said, "It can't be him."

Not knowing what else to do, Cindy put her arm around April and said, "Of course not. Let's go to Judith's and work this out together."

Bree stood for a moment longer, looking at the mirror in the same way that April had just done. She wanted what April said to be true. But she knew it wasn't. The question was, would she tell what she knew? Maybe not. Perhaps they would prove the case without her.

Nodding at herself in the mirror, Bree ran her fingers through her hair and straightened up. She could manage this the way she always had. What was important was helping April come to terms with what was happening.

But first, they needed to be safe from the storm.

"Bree?" Cindy asked from the door. "Are you okay?"

When she answered that yes she was, they both knew she was lying. But April didn't notice. She was too busy reliving every moment of her life with Ron and denying every possibility that Ron was responsible not only for Sara's disappearance, but for other women's, too.

"It's impossible," she mumbled.

Neither Bree nor Cindy answered her as they moved to Bree's car. But they were silent for different reasons. Cindy, because she wanted it to be true that it wasn't Ron, and Bree because she knew it was.

Forty Eight

R on woke, having felt as if he hadn't slept at all. But he had. Except nightmarish dreams had lasted all night, keeping him in that half-awake, half-asleep state. All he could remember was running. Hearing the word, run, and then running faster than he ever ran before. He felt exhausted from all that running.

Rolling over to sit on the edge of the bed, Ron slouched over, trying to ease his lower back pain. It came and went. Today it was worse. He hated that he was getting old. In his mind, he was ageless. His body didn't agree.

Still sitting on the bed, eyes closed so he wouldn't see his rounded stomach instead of the flat one he used to have, Ron drifted back in time to the fifteen-year-old boy who had just begun to discover his powers of persuasion. It had been heady and addicting. And over the years, he had developed and honed that skill to perfection. It was how he made his money.

But making money had never been enough. He knew himself well enough to know that he needed to feel important. Be important. And that involved more than persuading people in business. He had discovered the ecstasy of having power over people in all ways. The pleasure of using words that led to physical conquests. And through the years, he had gotten better at that, too.

At fifteen, he was still a nerdy teenager. But one day he had decided to make something of his life. To stop following and start leading. Stop being the victim of someone else's needs and desires and fulfill his own.

Glancing at his phone on the table beside the bed, he saw that April had called him again. Left no message. Just a call. She knew better than to disturb him when he was on a business trip. Which meant something was wrong.

Ron knew it was the feeling that something was wrong that had triggered the dreams. Ron sighed, hoping he was wrong. Although he had planned for years for the moment he had to run, he didn't want to. Planning was something he did for everything in life. Which meant he had plans for every contingency, just in case something went wrong. That planning included what he did on his business trips. Especially what he did on business trips.

Could this be the moment? He didn't want to believe it. Truthfully, he had thought this time would never come. He had been clever for years. No one knew the man he became when he was away from home. Over thirty-five years had gone by. Why now? How could someone figure out his secret?

It has to be something else, Ron thought as he ran through scenarios of what could have happened. Perhaps something happened to the kids, or even April? He shook his head at that thought. Something happening to April was a version of life Ron dreaded more than anything else. He loved April. He couldn't live without her. He always went home to her. April was his rock.

After his father left and then his mother died, he had thought he would live alone until that day he sat next to April in history class. She was a glowing light and when she turned her light towards him, he had felt as if his heart had moved out of his chest and into hers.

In all the years they had been together, she had shone that light on him. However, after his unexpected temper tantrum that caused her to move back to Spring Falls, he thought he had lost her. But using his power of persuasion, he won her back and now her light was shining brighter than ever.

Hearing her excitement about what she wanted to do with the house made him almost as happy as what he did when he was away. Almost.

Ignoring the phone, Ron rose. He'd take care of the business he had set up the day before and head home to hear what she had to say in person. Flipping on the TV to hear the news, he heard about the storm moving in south of where he was. Since it was passing directly over Spring Falls, the storm was probably what April was calling about.

But Ron knew April was safe with her friends, so there was nothing to worry about. He could go on with his day as planned, but instead of going back to Silver Lake when he finished his business, he'd head directly to Spring Falls and April. Hopefully, the storm would be over by then.

But still feeling uneasy, Ron retrieved his other phone from his suitcase and transferred a sizeable chunk of money to an account in one of his other names based in Canada. Just in case. It didn't hurt to be prepared.

Dressing, and packing his suitcase, Ron headed out into his day. It was all planned out. When he was done, he'd get rid of any evidence, including the false beard he was wearing, and head home.

The anticipation of what was to come chased away any lingering worries. For him, it was going to be a great day. What other people did with it wasn't his business.

Ron thought about calling April just to confirm that she was okay, but decided not to. It was not part of the plan, and it would make her think he was always available, destroying years of training.

Putting all thoughts of April out of his mind, Ron checked out of the hotel as one person and became another. It was temporary. He'd be back.

Forty Nine

M imi and Janet were still standing at the window, watching the snowfall growing thicker when a bolt of lightning flashed above them.

"Wow," Janet said.

At that moment, both their phones beeped. It was a message from Cindy to close the gallery and go home, or join them all at Judith's if they wanted to.

Mimi answered, saying that they'd come there. Should they bring food? Should they bring Mittens?

"Yes," Cindy wrote back.

"Whoa," Janet said. "Something's wrong."

"And it's not just this storm," Mimi answered. "Let's go!"

Working as a team, they found Mittens hiding under Cindy's desk. Taking an ice chest from the cupboard, they filled it with all the food in the refrigerator. They both kept a change of clothes at the gallery, and they had a go-bag in their car, so there was no reason to go home first to get anything.

The planning that had been done for times like this was all Mimi. She was always prepared. Claimed it was because she had been a girl scout, but Janet knew it was really because it was how she was. Mimi loved a challenge and wanted to always be ready for it.

As they moved swiftly through the gallery, Janet watched with admiration how Mimi made it all look so easy. If it was her, she'd probably still be looking for Mittens and what to put her in.

But with Mimi's skillful direction, they were packed and out the door in fifteen minutes. By then, there was already almost an inch of snow on the ground. Normally this would be nothing at all, just a beautiful winter snow. But they both knew because of the recent warm days, and moisture on the ground and on the roads, there would be ice underneath the snow. It was an invisible danger that would spell tragedy if they weren't careful.

Mimi had insisted on both of them putting chains on their shoes before stepping out of the door and within seconds Janet was grateful. She could feel the chains bite into the ice as they put everything into the car. Of course it had been Mimi who had discovered that there were slip on chains for shoes and insisted that they use them.

Another bolt of lightning ripped through the sky and within seconds, a clap of thunder.

"Wow." Janet said. "That was awesome!"

"Yes." Mimi said. "Let's go."

A second later, all the lights on the block flickered and went out. Street lights included. Mittens meowed from the back seat, and Janet said, "I know what you mean, Mittens."

Everything around the car was white. A thunderstorm white out. Beautiful and terrifying.

"Good thing Judith's house is not far," Mimi said. "But I'm going the back way to avoid the major intersections. People will not know how to stop."

205

As if she had prophesied it, there was a loud squeal of brakes and then a crash. Janet took out her phone and dialed 911 to report an accident downtown. She knew it was only the beginning.

In Doveland, hours away, Rachel and Bryan stood at their full-length window that faced the woods behind the house, watching the falling snow. Both of them were tired. In the past few days, Bryan had assisted one person after another to move on. Sometimes they would go weeks with no one asking for help, and then there would be so many people wandering in the in-between needing help neither of them got any rest.

It was why they had told Grace to let her friend in Spring Falls know they couldn't be there for a few days. They were in the middle of one of those times. Now the people were gone, but the snowstorm that had moved in was going to delay them.

Bryan had to admit he was grateful. He needed some quiet time and snow made for a quiet world. They were safe and warm, and together. Spring Falls could wait.

With his arm around her and seeing their reflection in the window, Bryan looked at Rachel, feeling, as he often did, a swelling of love for his wife. They had met in grade school, and he had fallen in love even then with the lighthearted, red-haired, green-eyed little girl.

They had dated in high school, but he was too afraid to tell her how much he loved her because he knew she was out of his league. Instead, he had moved away, trying to forget her and Doveland. Then his mother got sick, and he came home to take care of her. When she passed away, she left him the house.

His mother's death had opened the door to the in-between that he had firmly closed before. But with his mother's guidance from the in-between, he rescued one of her friends who had just passed away. In fact, he had helped that friend, Connie, go back in time, changing the ending of her life. Bryan still wasn't sure how that worked. But it did.

His mother had stayed until she was sure Bryan was comfortable doing this work and had gotten enough courage to tell Rachel how he felt. Luckily for him, she felt the same way, and they had married a year ago.

Now walking in the woods and being with Rachel were what sustained him, and gave him the courage to deal with those people that came to him for help.

Going to Spring Falls was a favor to Grace. He wasn't sure how he could help find a girl who had been missing for over thirty years. But stranger things had happened, and if he and Rachel could help, they would.

Rachel was watching the two of them in the reflection in the window, too. Being with Bryan had changed her life. Although she couldn't see the people in the in-between unless she was holding on to Bryan, she worked with him, sometimes seeing things he didn't see. But usually she was there just to support him. When Bryan didn't need her help, she worked as a real estate agent, helping people find their dream home. She supposed in some ways she and Bryan were in the same business. They both helped people find the perfect place for them to live.

"We are going to have to put off the trip to Spring Falls for a day or two," Bryan said.

Rachel nodded and leaned into him, feeling very grateful for the snow. She was looking forward to a few days of quiet. Then they would both be rested enough for an adventure in a new town. Grace said these were good people who needed their help. She was looking forward to a trip, meeting new people, and perhaps helping make their lives better.

Fifty

All the Ruby Sisters had a key to Judith's house, so Cindy unlocked the door as Bree supported a sagging April. The snow was falling so thickly by then they could barely see Mimi's car as it pulled up behind them.

"OMG," Janet said as she lifted Mittens out of the car, "This is crazy!"

"White out," Mimi said, as another lightning bolt flashed across the sky and thunder rumbled. Mimi grabbed their go-bag and the two of them carefully made their way up to the house.

They could hear the generator running that Judith had installed a few years before. It kicked on immediately when the power went out. She also had solar panels on her roof. They knew it was why Judith had told them all to go to her house. Like Mimi, she was always prepared. They'd be safe and warm there.

Bruce had followed Cindy, and knowing that Judith would still need to get into the garage, he pulled in behind Mimi's car, getting as close as he could. He didn't want to park at the curb because the snowplows would do their best to clear the roads, and his car would be in the way. Besides, if they didn't tow it away, it would be buried under piles of snow as they cleared the road.

When Nicky didn't move, he walked over to her door and gently helped her out of the car. Keeping his arm around her, he led her to the house. Marsha supported her on the other side.

"They are going to hate me, aren't they?" Nicky whispered.

"It will be okay," Bruce answered. He knew these women. They might be upset at first, but they would never let Nicky suffer more just because she was the one that told them about what she suspected.

If it was Ron, it wasn't her fault, and it was something they would have found out eventually. He hoped she was wrong, but no one seemed to think that she was. And the evidence was piling up against him. Was it something the Ruby Sisters had all suspected all along?

Bruce had only met the man once or twice. He was one of those people that Bruce thought of as a charmer. When he was younger, Bruce was envious of people like Ron. They knew all the right things to say. They always seemed to know when and how to smile at people to get what they wanted.

But as he got older, and worked with his clients, he learned that often charmers were people who hid their evil intentions behind their charm. So, even though he often wished he could be more outgoing and perhaps a tad charming himself, he no longer envied the charmers. Instead, he kept his distance.

So Ron, the charming man that he had been when they met, had raised his hackles just a bit. But knowing that Ron had been around the Ruby Sisters for years, he said nothing. He wondered if all of them had done the same thing. They were afraid of saying anything because April loved him.

If so, they were all going to have to talk about it now.

Inside, they all removed their shoes and hung up their wet coats, letting them drip onto the rubber trays that Judith kept by the door just for that purpose. Marsha kept her arm around Nicky and led her to the love seat, while Cindy guided April to the couch. Bruce and Bree headed into the kitchen to make coffee.

Once they were out of earshot, Bruce asked Bree, "Are you alright?"

Bruce knew Bree would view the situation through the lens of logic, but that didn't mean that it wasn't upsetting. And although Bree was always quiet, the intensity of her quiet at that moment made him think that something else was going on.

Bree looked at Bruce and sat down in one of the kitchen chairs, sighed, and shook her head.

"Secrets never stay secret, do they?"

Bruce sat down too, reaching out to touch Bree's hand. He knew she didn't like to be touched, Judith had warned him, and he understood. But at that moment, it felt like the right thing to do.

"Do you have a secret that needs to be told?"

"One I swore I would never tell."

"Are you thinking of telling it now?"

"I don't want to, but I am afraid that I will have to, because now it's the only right thing to do. I have never told it before, except to Paul. I have kept it secret because it is not only painful for me, but it could destroy other people's lives, too.

"And, truth be told, I thought people might not believe me. And then I would have ruined everything for nothing. Lose everyone."

"Is it why you moved away? Didn't you, in a way, lose everyone anyway?"

"I supposed I did. But part of me thought if I didn't tell, I could always come back. And I did. Now if I tell, it will be even more painful. Not only for me, but for many others. Honestly, I am not sure I can tell."

"Perhaps you could tell me. I will keep your secret, as Paul did, if that is what you wish. But at least you wouldn't be carrying it alone. Then, we can discuss it together. Decide what to do together."

Bree smiled at Bruce.

"I see why you have had such a successful business, and why Judith loves you."

Bruce's heart stopped beating for a second. Did Bree just say that Judith loved him? Was that true? How did Bree know?

Seeing his face flush, Bree smiled again. "What, you two haven't said those words to each other? Well, that is one secret now revealed."

Recovering, Bruce asked, "And yours?"

"You're right. It would help to tell you."

At that moment, they both heard the garage door open, and Bree sighed in relief. "But not right now. Perhaps later."

Bruce nodded and patted Bree's hand. "When you are ready, just give me a sign."

"I will. And Bruce, perhaps after all this is over, you and Judith need to have a little discussion too?"

"What do we need to discuss?" Judith asked, stepping into the kitchen. Although she had shed her coat, snowflakes coated her hair.

"It can wait," Bruce said, handing her a dishtowel. "Let's deal with what we have in front of us first."

Taking one look at Bree's face, Judith nodded.

"You're right. I brought pizza, and I got my computer from the office. Downtown is a mess. With the lights out, people do not know when and where to stop. I went the back way, but still ..."

"Shall we eat while the pizza is still slightly warm?" Bree asked.

"And pretend nothing is going on other than a snow thunderstorm?" Judith replied.

"Why not?" Cindy said, coming into the kitchen. "Let's delay the inevitable for just a few more minutes."

Bree watched, feeling a tightening in her chest. Yes, Cindy was right. The inevitable had come to pass. She would tell her secret. Not just to Bruce, to everyone.

The world had turned upside down for her friends, and she would just tilt it a little bit more. Bree was glad her daughter, Mary, was not there to hear what she had to say, although sooner or later she would have to tell her.

But she hoped it wasn't today.

Fifty One

The world had stopped. Or at least that's what it felt like to Judith. Although the power came back on before everyone went to bed, the snow kept falling and falling. Everything outside her window was white. The only color was the holiday decorations' faint blotches of light shining far behind their coating of snow.

It was a wet snow, which meant branches bent and some broke under the weight. The only sounds besides the occasional cracking branch were the snow plows that kept clearing a street that would fill up an hour later. Once in a while, a car would struggle by, and Judith wondered what could be so important that they had ventured out into the storm.

To Judith, the best part of the storm was the quiet. And that it had brought all of her friends under one roof. They were safe. She didn't know what they were safe from yet, but she knew that if they were in her house, she could watch over them.

After their lunch of pizza and ice cream, Judith suggested a nap for everyone. If she had intended to make everyone sleepy, it had worked. Except for her. Her mind would not stop working, even with the overload of carbs and sugar.

Judith had given her bedroom to Mimi and Janet. Bree was sharing with Marsha, and Cindy with April. Both Bruce and Nicky had their own room. Judith had a couch in her office, which she often used to take quick naps. Today she made it through a five-minute nap before waking up, her mind filled with questions. And she wanted answers.

And if not answers, solutions. Because if it was Ron who was responsible for all these missing women, and he found out that they knew, what would he do? For Judith, hearing that Nicky, and now Booker, believed it to be true that it was Ron, everything fell into place.

His long trips away where no one knew where he was. The mysteries surrounding everything he did. And then the fact that she never fully trusted him, but hadn't understood why.

There was a tap on her office door, and Bruce peeked into the room. Mittens streaked through and then wound herself around Judith's legs. Picking her up, Judith sat down on her office couch put her on her lap, and patted the seat beside her for Bruce.

It always surprised Judith how delighted she was to see Bruce. She had been self sufficient for so long she thought she wouldn't enjoy having someone in her space. But Bruce was different. He didn't take up her space. Somehow, he opened it up.

And despite why he was there, his presence made her happy. *Someday I'll have to tell him,* Judith thought. *But not today.*

However, when he turned to look at her, she realized she might not have to tell him. He probably already knew.

"Want to talk?" Bruce asked. "I have a few questions. Perhaps it's easier for me since I am an outsider, but there are a few things that don't make sense to me."

"Like what?"

"Well, for one, how Ron could have pulled this—whatever it is—off for all these years? Didn't you all suspect him?"

Judith paused, chewing her lip before answering. "I think we didn't want to believe that something was wrong. Although I was always uneasy around him, I thought it could just be me. Besides, why would we assume he was doing something this bad?

"And we didn't really know him. He took April away, and we didn't see them for the over thirty years. That's a long time. April and I talked almost every week, but she only told me the good parts about her life and the kids. It wasn't until Paul's letter arrived after he died that we all got back together and saw Ron again.

"But yes, I have always felt there was something off about Ron. But what? Aren't we all a little 'off' in other people's eyes?"

Bruce nodded, agreeing, but thinking that he saw nothing off about Judith. Watching her hold Mittens, her soft red hair lit up by the lamp behind her, he wanted to blurt out what he felt. Once again, he wondered if Paul had known that he would fall for Judith. Was it why he had chosen him to be his attorney?

What else did Paul know? Bruce wondered.

As if she was reading his mind, Judith asked, "Do you think Paul knew about Ron?"

"I think he suspected what Ron was doing," Bree said, standing in the doorway. "But it was my secret he was keeping, so he couldn't say anything. His letter keeps on giving, doesn't it?

"And now that it appears Ron has been doing evil things for a long time, I think it's time to tell that secret to the two of you. Then perhaps you can help me figure out a way to tell everyone else."

Thinking about who she'd have to tell, Bree felt as if she would be sick.

Judith stood and embraced Bree, and Bree let her.

Gesturing to the small round table she used with clients who came to her home office, Judith said, "Let's sit here. Do you want anything to drink?"

Bree shook her head, no. She didn't want to be distracted. It was time to tell.

Once they were all seated, Mittens jumped up onto Bree's lap, turned around in circles before settling in and purring softly, helping Bree feel a tiny bit safer.

Taking a deep breath, she said, "Ron is why we left Spring Falls after our wedding and why we never came back."

"Oh, Bree," Judith said, seeing the obvious now that it was staring her in the face. She should have known. How could she have missed this and then let her friend suffer all these years.

Her eyes filled with tears, she said, "He's Mary's father, isn't he?"

Bree nodded, tears streaming down her cheeks. She wasn't sure if it was because of the relief of finally telling someone, or the fear of what it meant, or the regret for not saying it before. Because, feeling Judith's support, she knew it was exactly how everyone would have acted if she would have just told them. She could have saved herself years of pain. And what if she would have told everyone years ago? Would Ron have been stopped then?

Sighing again, she said, "But I didn't know it was him at first. He wore a mask and gloves. It happened in an alley when I was coming home from one of my jobs. I was too terrified to move, because he showed me a knife and I knew he would use it if I resisted.

"He didn't speak as it happened. Later, playing it over and over in my head I eventually realized who it was because I recognized how he moved. Since he whispered as he left that if I told anyone what had happened he would kill me, I didn't.

"Until I discovered I was pregnant. I knew it wasn't Paul's because we had chosen not to have sex again for a few months before our marriage. Crazy to think that was a romantic thing to do. Stupid right?

"Of course, I had to tell Paul. Well, I didn't have to. I thought of disappearing, but he figured out something was wrong and made me tell him. He didn't want me to give up the baby. But I insisted. I insisted that he not tell. I insisted we move away.

"I was such a self-centered fool," Bree said.

Judith said nothing, just stood and pulled Bree up into a hug, and then held her as she sobbed. Mittens, no longer needed, sauntered out of the room, squeezing through the small opening. Over Bree's head, Judith looked at Bruce, and he nodded, thinking the same thing. If Ron only raped women, why were they missing? Or was Bree left alive because she was April's friend? Or had he not escalated yet? Was that good news for Sara?

As Mittens slid out the door, she brushed against the legs of someone slumped against the wall beside the door. Someone, having heard Bree's story, stood silently sobbing, wondering what to do. Tell or not?

Not, Marsha decided, as she tiptoed back up to her room. Now they knew for sure what Ron was, she didn't need to tell them what she knew. It was her secret and she was keeping it.

Fifty Two

*W*ell, *that wasn't satisfying,* Ron thought as he gripped the steering wheel, trying to calm himself down. Everything had gone wrong that day. The woman had not turned up where she was expected.

Normally he would have checked into another hotel, and waited for another day or another woman. This time, he couldn't. He had to get home and get April.

What really pissed him off was that he knew he was making a terrible decision, but he couldn't stop himself from doing it. Instead of heading south to Spring Falls, he should head north. He'd be over the border within an hour. He could start a new life. One that he had long ago planned. There was plenty of money and even forged documents waiting for him. He could go anywhere and be anyone. Start over. Satisfy himself.

But instead, against his good judgment, he was heading south, straight into the storm, and probably straight into a danger that he didn't need to put himself in. *Stupid, stupid,* he said to himself. He was angry and upset for all the reasons he knew he shouldn't be. He had better self-control than that.

But he couldn't leave April. He had to get her and take her with him. He'd explain. She'd understand, and if she didn't, he'd make her understand.

Ron brushed his hair out of his eyes and gripped the steering wheel tighter, wishing he could have flown instead of driving. Because of the storm, there were no planes flying, and he didn't have the time to wait for the weather to clear. Stealing a car and switching license plates had been easy. It was a skill he had learned through the years, and a rule he made and never broke. Never a rental. Never his car. Never keep it.

The pines and trees were thick on either side of the lane. Night was coming, but it was still light enough to see. There was a faint orange glow from the sun as it sank in the west. He was still far enough above the storm that there was only a small sprinkling of falling snow. He figured that once he got to Spring Falls, the worst part of the storm would be over, and the snowplows would have had plenty of time to clear the roads.

As he drove, Ron relived the past thirty-five years of his life. He had never regretted a single moment of it. Once he allowed himself to take control of his life, everything had gone as planned. He had the wife and kids. He had a wildly successful business. And he had a life on the side that had both challenged him and satisfied him in ways that neither his family nor business life could do.

It pleased him that he felt nothing for what he had done other than satisfaction. Yes, he knew what that made him, but did he care? Not a bit. All he had cared about was keeping April with him and making her happy. And that had been a piece of cake until Paul wrote that damn letter and upset everything.

Now, he was sure that all the Ruby Sisters had finally figured it out. And he hadn't understood how that could be until he listened to April's message. He could barely hear her. All she said was that someone named Nicky had come to town and said things that scared her.

"Ron, please tell me you don't know what I am talking about," she had whispered. "Please call and make it all okay again."

The trouble is, Ron thought. *I do know what she is talking about. Nicky. Sara's sister. It's where it all began, and now it all must end. At least here. We'll start over.*

"I'll fix it, April," he said out loud to himself. "We'll go away and start over."

As he got closer to Spring Falls, he held the steering wheel even tighter. The road was slippery, and he could feel the tires not gripping the road the way they should. This was a dangerous thing he was doing. Driving in the dark through a storm. Going back to a town where he knew he would be detained if he they saw him.

Everything about his life right now was like the road, slippery and dangerous. But he had to get April.

He had finally texted her when he had stopped for gas. He told her he was on the way to Spring Falls and had a surprise for her. Could she meet him at their new house but keep it a secret?

"Why a secret?"

"It's a surprise just for you. Can you get there?"

"Why the house? There's a storm outside!"

"Okay, not the house. I'll text you when I am in town and you can slip out and we'll go to the house together."

"Maybe." April had texted back.

That was good enough for Ron. It had to be.

"I love you, April," he had responded.

"Maybe," she had answered.

Praying that he was in time, that April wouldn't tell anyone their plans because she loved him, praying that he could get her into his car, Ron kept his eyes on the road, held the steering wheel steady and planned what to do in case none of that happened.

He had already removed everything from his luggage that would incriminate him in the slightest. They would have nothing on him, and after stopping him, would have to let him go. Of course, this wasn't his car, but as soon as he got to town, he'd find another car and ditch this one in case they were already tracking this one, so he would be safe there, too.

That was the worse case scenario.

No, he said to himself. *That is not the worse case scenario. That would be if I can't take April with me. That would be bad. Very bad.* So he couldn't, and wouldn't, fail.

April moved quietly, being careful not to wake Cindy. Her clothes were lying on top of the covers where she had peeled them off, too tired to do anything else but strip them off her.

She slipped her clothes on under the covers and she checked her phone one last time. Ron was only a few minutes away.

Making as little sound as possible, she grabbed her purse off the floor and tiptoed downstairs, grateful for Judith's diligence. There were no squeaking stairs or doors, but a stair light flicked on, enabling her to see where she was going.

At the front door, she slipped on her coat and shoes and stepped outside where it was so white she felt as if the clouds had descended to earth and she had stepped inside of them. The air smelled clean and crisp, the cold making the inside of her nose tingle.

Someone had shoveled off the porch and made a path down the driveway past the parked cars, now buried under mounds of snow, making it easy to get to the street.

The moon hung heavy and deep in the sky, giving her just enough light to see. The snow had stopped. The storm was over. All of this, April took as a sign that this was what she was supposed to be doing.

She'd explain later to the Ruby Sisters, but first she had to hear what Ron had to say.

A car moved slowly and stealthily down the street and rolled gently to a stop in the middle of the street. Ron stepped out, leaving the door open.

April's heart thudded in her chest. This was Ron. The man she had married so many years ago. They had children together. He could not be what they said.

Ron reached her and they hugged, both of them trembling.

Without speaking, Ron helped April into the car, slid into the driver's seat and they glided silently away into the white world.

Fifty Three

That night, Janet and Mimi had suggested watching a movie together. They made popcorn and tried their best to make it a good evening. But even though everyone watched the movie, most of them barely touched the popcorn, just stared at the screen saying nothing.

Marsha stayed by Nicky, who looked like she wanted to disappear, and probably would have if there wasn't a storm outside. Cindy stayed by April, who looked the same way. Neither of them acknowledged the other.

"At least Judith and Bruce seemed okay," Janet said to Mimi later as they crawled into bed.

"And Bree. Not okay, but different," Janet added.

"Mmmm," Mimi said as she slid over in bed to snuggle with Janet.

Within minutes, they were both asleep and, like most of the rest of the house, didn't wake until the sun beamed through the curtain in their window.

It wasn't until after everyone had made it down to coffee and blueberry pancakes made by Bruce that they noticed April's absence.

"I looked over at the bed, but she was still sleeping," Cindy said. "I thought the sleep would do her good."

Judith took one look at Bruce and then raced up the stairs. In the room, she found pillows under the covers, not April. Bruce and Bree were right behind her, and the three of them stared at the empty bed.

It was Bree who said what they were all thinking. "Ron."

"We don't know that for sure," Marsha said as they came downstairs and reported what they found.

"Where else would she be? And if not Ron, why hide that she was gone?" Bree said.

"It's all my fault," Nicky mumbled, standing, the chair banging the floor as it fell over, making everyone jump.

"Not," Marsha said. Everyone nodded in agreement, but Nicky, ever aware of how other people felt even when they didn't speak, knew that some of them were wishing she had never come to town. Wished she had never told them what she knew. Wondered why she couldn't have just left it alone.

She should have known better. Sara being missing was her pain. She shouldn't have brought it to them. And now their friend was with that monster.

Stop feeling sorry for yourself, Nicky thought to herself. *After tracking him for all these years, you know Ron's habits the best. Where is he going?*

"Sorry," Nicky said as she picked the chair off the floor. "Let me help. Can we call Booker? I think I know where Ron is going."

"I'll call," Bree said, reaching for her phone.

"Look," Judith said, holding out her phone. "You're right, she went with him."

Judith passed her phone to Bruce, and they watched as April walked down the driveway and into Ron's car. The time on the camera showed it had happened over five hours before.

"Why would she do that?" Cindy asked.

"Love. Or habit. Or wishful thinking," Judith answered "After all this time, how can she admit she didn't know her husband? Or that she did, and didn't want to see what was happening. It's hard for all of us. Imagine what it's like for her."

"Do we contact their kids? Would they be going there?" Marsha asked.

"He'd never go to the kids," Judith answered. "He barely acknowledges them. No, he is probably taking her out of the country, heading north. It's closest. And if he has been doing this for years, he is a planner. He made plans for something like this. We just have to stop him before he takes April where we can't find her, or he hurts her."

"And someday he will," Nicky said. "Once she realizes the truth about him, he'll think she betrayed him."

"Agreed," Judith said, thinking that it was good that Nicky was coming alive. They would need what she knew. They'd find April. They'd turn the world upside down to do it if necessary.

"Where are you, April?" she texted. "You are missing Bruce's blueberry pancakes."

When there was no answer, she slapped her forehead. She had made all the Ruby Sisters put the Find My Friend app on their phone. They would track her that way.

So excited that her hands were trembling, she opened the app. April was still there, but it said "location not available."

April would not have turned off her phone. Ron had.

By the time Booker arrived at the house, everyone was dressed and ready to help with the search. To their disappointment, Booker told them there was nothing to do. He had already sent out a BOLO, which included both Ron and April's picture. April's car was still in the garage, having been blocked in by Bree and Bruce's car, so they were looking for Ron's car.

"But what if he stole one?" Marsha asked.

"Possible. But it doesn't matter. We'll find them. In the meantime, keep trying to reach April. We'll try tracking her phone. It's possible it's just the app that is turned off and not her phone. And perhaps, pray," Booker added. "Whatever that means to you."

After Booker left, Judith said, "Let's do what he asked. But it will not do any good sitting around here worrying. I'm going into the office. Can I take anyone with me? Other than Bruce," she added, glancing his way. "I have some people there we can contact."

"May I go with you?" Nicky asked. "I might be able to help?"

Getting an affirmative nod from Judith, she headed upstairs to get her purse.

Watching her leave the room, Cindy sighed. Nicky had uprooted their entire lives, but there was no reason to blame her. Secrets have to be told. Otherwise, it was like a festering wound that no one notices until it's too late. All they could do was pray that it wasn't too late for April.

Turning to Mimi and Janet, she asked, "Could you two give Marsha and me a ride to my house, and then I'll meet you and Mittens at the gallery once I get cleaned up?"

"Sure, we're ready whenever you are."

As the four of them headed upstairs to get their clothes, Bree turned to Bruce and Judith.

"I need to go to see Mary," Bree said.

"Do you want company?" Judith asked.

"No, this is something I need to do by myself. This is one mess I have control over. I have to hope that Mary understands. If not, then I pray she forgives me someday. But I need to start that healing process now."

227

"You did nothing wrong," Judith said. "It wasn't your fault it happened."

"But it was my fault for not telling. I might have saved lives. For sure, Paul and I could have raised a child together. There is nothing I can do about that past, but I can make a difference now."

"If you need us, we are always here for you," Judith said, waving her hand to include all the people upstairs.

"I know. And it's something my younger self should have realized. I have to admit, I am as terrified now as I was then. Maybe even a little more, because now I know what I could lose when I tell this secret to Mary and Seth. But I have to do it. I'll tell the rest of the Ruby Sisters after we bring April home."

From your lips to God's ear, Judith thought to herself, adding, "Come back to us, April," to her prayer.

She hoped that both God and April were listening, but she would not waste time wishing and hoping. She was going to do something.

As Bruce shoveled the snow away from the bottom of the driveway, she cleaned the kitchen. By the time he was done, and everyone had driven away, she had changed clothes and she and Nicky were ready to go.

"Coming for you, April," Judith said to the mirror as she checked her reflection one last time.

For a moment Judith thought she heard a voice that sounded just like Paul say, "I'll help," but shrugged it off, thinking it was just her imagination. But then she stopped and said out loud, in case it wasn't.

"I'll take it. Thanks!"

Fifty-Four

Nothing could have prepared April for how she felt sitting next to Ron as he focused on the road ahead, barely talking. Not that she hadn't tried to get him to talk.

As soon as they got into the car, she started asking questions. Simple ones. Not the hard one about what people thought he had done.

Instead, she asked questions about what was happening at that moment, as if it was normal to be sneaking out in the middle of the night. She smiled and asked, "Why the secrecy? Where are we going? Why did he drive to Spring Falls during a storm to get her?"

He had answered the last one. In fact, he had pulled over and reached out to hug her the best that he could across the console of the car.

"I missed you so much, April."

April hugged him back, thinking about how wonderful it felt, pushing away all thoughts that Ron was anything other than a workaholic husband who was rarely home. Together, they would figure out how to prove this to everyone else.

"Missed you, too," she answered truthfully. Smiling, she asked again where they were going since they appeared to be driving in a direction away from her new house.

"I thought we'd go on a trip together," Ron answered, smiling shyly at her and then glancing back to the road. "I know you don't have your stuff with you, but we can buy you all new things. Won't that be fun?"

"Sure. I guess," April answered, still holding her smile. "But let me tell everyone what's happening so they don't worry."

As April pulled out her phone, Ron grabbed it from her, turned it off and dropped it in the door pocket beside him.

Then, and only then, did April allow herself to wonder if Ron was not who she thought he was, but was the man that Nicky said he was. She couldn't stop herself now. She needed to know, so she started asking more questions. And Ron stopped answering them.

Calming herself, April tried another way, thinking that perhaps her rising hysteria was affecting him, too.

"Sorry, Ron. You know I am just your curious little wren. This is quite an adventure. I was just wondering what I needed to know about it."

And then, knowing how important it was for Ron to feel valuable, she fed his ego as she had all the days of her marriage. Not for the reason she did then, to ensure his happiness, which made her happy, but because she finally understood that it might be the only way to ensure her safety.

Remembering the day he had thrown everything in the refrigerator onto the floor, she knew that buried beneath the independent but accommodating husband was an angry man. The last thing she needed was for him to lose his temper while she was trapped in the car with him.

Her appeasing seemed to work. Ron smiled as he agreed that they were going on an adventure together.

But when April asked him again if he could tell her where they were going, he stopped smiling and clutched the steering wheel so hard his knuckles turned white.

April patted his hand, smiling as sweetly as she could, and said, "Sorry, Ron. It's okay, I like surprises."

Seeing Ron's hands relax, April leaned back in her seat and closed her eyes, willing herself to calm down. Breathe the way Judith had taught her. She imagined herself back in Cindy's gallery the first day she had returned to Spring Falls, felt again the joy of meeting Janet and Mimi, and the peace of holding Mittens as she purred her welcome.

It worked. She calmed down. Keeping her eyes closed, she reached her thoughts out to each member of the Ruby Sisters and showed them a picture of where she was and who she was with. Sure, she knew she was simply imagining something, and there was probably no way they would know what she was telling them. But then, what else could she do?

Besides, she had heard that such things could work. There were stranger things that happened, weren't there? Sometimes she knew when the phone was going to ring, and who was calling before she looked.

Besides the imagining, the visualizing, was keeping her calm, and she knew that was what she needed to do. Keep calm. Don't make Ron mad.

When she opened her eyes thirty minutes later she realized that the sun was up, shining bravely through the clouds and they were no longer in town. Instead, they were on a highway in what felt like the middle of nowhere. She could see only a few cars on the road, and snow covered everything except for the cleared lane on the road.

"Did you have a nice nap?" Ron asked, smiling kindly at her.

"Um, yes, I did, thank you," April answered, feeling the terror surge through her body again. How had she never noticed Ron's strange moods before? How easily he had moved from that steely anger to this sugary sweet voice?

Perhaps he had never shown his true self to me before, she thought. But if he was letting his guard down now, it probably meant he wasn't expecting her to be anywhere again but with him.

Forcing the rising hysteria down, she said, "Hey, hon, when we get a chance, can we stop somewhere to eat? I'm starving. And besides, I have to use the bathroom.

"Sure, I'll find us a rest stop."

Reaching behind him, still keeping his eyes on the road, Ron grabbed a cold bag from behind April's seat and handed it to her.

"Here you go, love. I made you your favorite sandwich and brought your favorite drink."

April peeked in the bag and realized he had indeed made her favorite sandwich and brought her favorite drink. Since when had he known what she liked? Since when had he made her a sandwich?

It was with the realization that he had always just taken what he wanted, and that doing this now was only a form of control, making it impossible for her to get away from him, that she finally accepted what she had been afraid of all along. But not allowed herself to believe.

Ron had kidnapped her, and she had let it happen. Now she knew she would probably never see her kids again. Never do something with the house he bought her. Never see any of her friends again.

It was only the terror of what Ron would do if she screamed or cried that kept her silent. Now her fate was entirely in his hands. She was trapped. Her life was over one way or another.

What made it worse was she realized that only since returning to Spring Falls had she just begun to live a life she wanted. Now all her dreams were gone. How stupid she had been. But it was too late to fix it now.

Fifty Five

As she filled the customers' coffee cup, Jane heard the name Ron Page, and almost dropped the pot.

"You okay, miss?" the man asked.

"Sorry, just clumsy today," Jane said, and reaching for the remote, turned up the TV broadcasting an interview with a tall woman, with soft red hair and blue eyes. She was standing in front of a police station talking about her friend being taken by her husband.

"Ah, geez," the man said, glancing up at the TV. "It's just some hysterical woman worried about nothing."

Jane couldn't help herself. She snapped back, "Or it could be something. Men don't own women, you know!"

The man stood, slammed some money down, grabbed his coat and hat and stepped out into the cold white world. This was not the place he wanted to be, with some damn old angry woman.

Outside, the winter storm was over, and roads were being cleared. However, it would be days before it melted. And before it did, it would turn into a gray, slushy mess. A thing of dangerous beauty turning ugly. *Like life*, Jane thought.

She got a small tinge of pleasure watching the man trying to balance his heavy belly over his feet as he slipped his way to his car parked outside. She didn't want him to fall, but she enjoyed watching him struggle.

What did he know about the perils of being a woman?

Jane grabbed the money he left, walked back into the kitchen, and leaned against the wall, breathing heavily, tears running down her cheeks. After all these years, and now Ron Page had shown up again. She had no doubt it was the same man the red-haired woman was describing. Although the Ron Page she knew was a boy the last time she saw him, she knew it was him. It was the boy turned into a man. Still up to his evil.

But what could she do? She had not done something years before. Why now? She was a coward. She knew that. It was why she had run away instead of staying and facing the looks she would have gotten. Who would she have told? People would not have believed her, anyway.

The only person who might have understood was her sister. But her sister had left home, so she was of no help to her at all. Yes, she had been a coward. But that was then. What was she now?

Sliding down the wall to the sticky floor, Jane dropped her head to her knees and thought about her life. The tiny, useless life she lived for all these years. She was going to be someone. And then she ran away because she was afraid.

Considering how hard it was to be fifteen and on the road, and what she had to do to survive, it was almost funny. It would have been so much easier to stay and live that life than the one she had.

She had let herself down, and now years later there he was, probably doing evil the whole time she was running. She might have been able to stop it. At least she could have tried. She was not only a coward, she was selfish.

Standing, she brushed herself off, looked around at the kitchen, that looked like so many she had been in before, and sighed. Then something rose up inside of her. Maybe it was anger at what that man had said, but whatever it was, she was tired of who she had become and ready to do something about it.

For all these years, she had let herself remain a victim. It was time to change that. It was time to find the part of herself that had once been strong and believed in a happy life. She might never have that life, but perhaps she could help someone else experience it.

The woman on the TV mentioned Spring Falls. She knew where Spring Falls was. She could go there. No one would know her. She could remain anonymous. Become a new person. *Yes,* Jane decided. She'd go to Spring Falls and see if there was something she could do to help while not revealing who she used to be.

Standing, she brushed herself off and wiped her eyes with the corner of her apron. It was time to move on again, anyway. And somehow, after all these years, she had circled back to being only an hour away from where the monster on the news was, the one she had met all those years ago and who had ruined her life. It was a sign.

Sighing again, she thought about what she was thinking of doing, and reminded herself that going to Spring Falls didn't mean she had to reveal who she was. She'd just go and see if there was any way to help.

It would be easy. Her latest paycheck was in her purse. There was no one in the restaurant. A snow day was keeping everyone home. The timing was perfect.

Hanging her apron on a hook by the door, she grabbed her coat and purse, walked into the owner's office and said, "I'm sorry Gerry, I have to go home. It's an emergency."

Gerry, who had never heard Jane mention a home or family, opened his mouth to say something and decided not to. He knew a determined woman when he saw one. Instead he nodded and said, "Good luck."

"Thank you," Jane said, gently closing the door behind her.

I'll need it, she thought. *And perhaps after all this time I might for once have some. Or at least bring it to someone else. That would be good enough.*

Fifty Six

"What did she say?" Judith asked, pulling Bree into a hug. Bree didn't resist. She felt as if she had used up every last bit of energy talking to Mary and Seth, and she was happy to soak up some of Judith's energy.

Judith was like a live wire. It was as if everything going on around her ignited a fire in her. Judith crackled with determination.

Not for the first time, Bree thought about how grateful she was for meeting Judith and all the other Ruby Sisters. Who knew that finding each other in grade school would lead to a day like this? No one.

"She said she understood. But how could she really? It's hard enough to finally learn your father's name, but to find out on the day the world learns he is a monster? How can she understand that?"

Bree sat down in the chair opposite Judith's desk, letting herself sag into it. The relief enveloping her was almost as enormous, as the guilt she felt at telling Mary so late in her life and on a day like this. What she wanted to do was go home and lie down and cry the way she did when Paul died. Maybe disappear for a month or two.

But today was not the day. No one had died. And there were more important things going on. Their friend was missing. Today, they all needed to put aside all of their fears and personal feelings to find April and bring her safely home.

"But the weirdest thing happened. I kept thinking that Paul was sitting beside me as I told them. I could almost feel his relief. For me. For Mary. I know that's impossible, but it felt good anyway. It helped, even if it was just my imagination."

Judith glanced up at Bruce, who had heard the last part of what Bree said. He winked at her in response. She had told Bruce that she thought she had heard Paul say he would help. Yes, Paul seemed to be everywhere. Were they all going crazy?

Maybe Grace's friends, Bryan and Rachel, can answer that question, Judith thought to herself. They had texted earlier that now that the storm was over, they were on their way. It didn't seem like a great time to be hosting people, but she didn't want to turn them away now.

"Speaking of Paul, Grace's friends will be here this afternoon. Could they stay at your place?"

Judith knew Bree preferred to be alone, but who could be picky at this point?

"Sure," Bree answered. "In the meantime, what can I do?"

"Nothing really," Booker answered, stepping into the room.

Judith thought that perhaps if all these people continued to come to her, she would need a bigger office. And then when her assistant, Nancy, poked her head in the door to announce a client she had forgotten about, she was sure of it.

Or at the very least, use the conference room, she told herself. Somehow, in the past few months, her life had exploded with people. She loved it. But something had to change.

Looking up at Bruce, he got the message and ushered Nicky, Booker, and Bree out of the room.

Once Judith's client went into her office and the door was closed, Booker turned to the three of them.

"As you know, we released a BOLO yesterday for Ron. Judith's interview went out to all the local stations. Nothing yet, but we won't stop until we find Ron and April."

"I'll stay here and help Judith with whatever she needs." Bruce said.

"I think I'll head over to the Gallery and make myself useful there," Nicky said, waving goodbye as she stepped outside into the snow, pulling her coat around her, being careful not to slip. Bree had the fleeting thought that she needed to buy Nicky a warmer coat and some snow boots. She added that to her growing list of things she needed to do.

"Shall we go get coffee, Bree?" Booker asked.

Her heart thudded a beat before nodding yes and shrugged on the coat he held out to her.

Once they were gone, Bruce let out a breath he didn't know he was holding and sat down to wait for Judith. He felt incredibly useless, but he knew he was where he needed to be. In fact, the more time he spent in Spring Falls, the more he felt as if it was where he needed, and wanted, to stay.

But he didn't want to stay at Judith's. Whatever their relationship was going to be, he didn't want it to be muddled by being too close together all the time. It was time to find a place of his own in Spring Falls and see what happened from there.

There was a real estate office next door. He had time to talk to them.

"Would you tell Judith to text me when she's done?" He asked Nancy.

A few minutes later, he was explaining what he needed to the woman behind the desk and feeling as if a weight had lifted off of him. Yes, although he had decided before to come to Spring Falls, today he was doing something more about it.

At the coffee shop Booker and Bree stared at each other, a scone broken in half, lying in front of them, both of them trying to figure out what to say.

They each knew that the most important thing in their lives right now was finding April. However, they had a history hanging between them that had to be addressed.

It was Bree who spoke.

"It seems this is the day secrets are being told. I did one of the hardest things I have ever done today. I told Mary that Ron was her father, and how it happened. And now that I did that, it's your turn. You need to explain something to me.

"I know it was a long time ago. We were only in high school and just kids. But I had such a huge crush on you, and I thought you had one on me. And then one day you ignored me, and it was over.

"I am so tired of secrets. Mine. Ron's. Yours. I know you are exhausted, but sometimes that makes it easier to let go. Tell me, Booker, why did you treat me that way?"

Booker put his coffee down and reached across the table to hold Bree's hand. He did not know why he had let this fester so long. It was such a small thing in the scheme of things, and it had only grown this big because he had never told her what had happened.

Bree smiled at Booker as he started to speak.

And then both their phones rang.

Fifty Seven

This time, they were not all sitting in the hospital room waiting for a baby to be born, as they were only a few months before.

This time, a week before Christmas, they were in the hospital waiting to find out if their friend would live.

They were taking turns sitting by April's side, holding her hand, telling her everything would be okay. So far, nothing. April lay still. Barely breathing.

"It's her decision to wake up or not," the doctors had told them.

All they knew was someone in a passing car had seen a body lying by the side of the road and called for help.

April had bruises all over her body and a gash on her head. Other than that, she was fine. Except she wouldn't wake up.

"She was lucky." the doctor said. "She was wearing a coat and hat. That helped."

"Helped how?" Cindy had sobbed out, barely able to speak.

All of them had gathered around the doctor to hear his conjecture that she had thrown herself out of a moving car.

He added that the snowbank on the side of the road had also cushioned her fall. Yes, it all helped her from dying on the road.

No one spoke after that. Holding hands, they stood together, imagining the terror that April must have felt that forced her to do something that dangerous.

"It was her only way out," Marsha whispered, and they all nodded in agreement.

Booker was not in the waiting room. He was busy looking for Ron. His fury at what had happened matched only by their grief.

Although Mary, Seth, Mimi, and Janet had been told of April's return, Judith had asked them to stay where they were. Pray in whatever way worked for them. Baby Rho and the gallery needed to be attended to. She'd call when there was news.

But Judith hadn't known what to do with Rachel and Bryan other than bring them to the hospital with them. They had arrived a few hours before they found April and they had not had time or energy to find somewhere else for them to go.

Bryan and Rachel sat a little off to the side, Rachel holding tightly to Bryan's arm, watching the twinkling lights of the Christmas tree in the corner.

"Are you doing okay?" Rachel asked Bryan. A hospital was not Bryan's favorite place to be. Too many people in the in-between hung out at a hospital. There were dead people visiting family and friends. Others who had died and didn't know it yet, or didn't want to accept it. And still others trying to decide whether to stay or go.

As she held onto Bryan's arm, Rachel could see some of them leaning against the wall and walking the hallway outside the waiting room. She didn't want to see them, but at the same time, she didn't want to let go of Bryan. She knew he needed her to keep him grounded, and she would never let him down if she could help it.

So she calmed her trembling, took a deep breath, and told herself to not look. She couldn't do anything for them, she could only help Bryan.

"We could wait somewhere else. A hotel room or something?" Bryan shook his head. "I can't leave."

"Too many people want your help?" Rachel whispered back.

"No, it's not that. I can tell them I'm busy. It's these people's friend, April. She hasn't come here with her body. I have to help her return to herself. Do you think they would let me go in the room alone with her?"

Rachel glanced over at the other woman with red hair. She wondered if her red hair would soften to the same lovely shade as she got a little older. Judith looked back at her and raised her eyebrows. Rachel tilted her head toward the open door, whispered she'd be right back to Bryan, and stepped outside.

Judith joined her a moment later.

"Do you think Bryan could spend a moment with April? Alone? I know it's hard to understand, or maybe even believe, but he has this gift. And I think he can bring April back to you."

Without warning, Judith's eyes filled with tears, catching her completely by surprise. She hadn't known how helpless she felt until that moment. Whatever it took, she was willing.

"He can?"

"He thinks he can. It's up to her, but he can help."

A few minutes later, Bryan stood in April's room, holding her hand. She wasn't there. She was still back on the side of the road. Filled with pain. Not just the physical pain, but the pain of seeing her life for what it had been. The man she loved was a monster. *How could I have loved him?* April kept asking herself. *How could I have not known?*

Bryan held her physical hand while cradling April at the side of the road as she told him what happened.

Bryan learned that April now knew everything about Ron, because Ron had told her the truth. He had told her how it started. And how it grew into more than just a physical assault because eventually he needed more. He needed to see and feel the control of each woman's life. He told her how much he loved being there when their life drained out of them.

Once Ron started telling her his secrets, he couldn't stop. His face lit up. His body trembled with excitement and joy.

"Finally, I can share myself with you," he had said. He was so excited that he was completely oblivious to what he was doing to his wife.

April had listened, frozen in place. Too terrified to say anything, or even react.

Ron interpreted her silence to mean she understood. The dam of secrets had broken open and words tumbled out of his mouth like a tidal wave, sweeping away everything April had known. April let herself drown in the wave of fear, willed herself to not move, to stay silent.

But when Ron said, "Then there was Bree and .....," April broke.

"No more," she had shouted, as she opened the door and threw herself out onto the road. All she wanted to do was die. She was shocked and disappointed that she hadn't. There was no way she could live with what Ron told her and how, because she was such an idiot, she had been a part of it. She should have known.

So she was still lying by the side of the road, waiting for death to come take her away.

Bryan waited until she told him the whole story. He helped her release all the poison Ron had shown her until it was gone. Then he guided her back to her body, reminding her that she had friends who needed her. That there was a new life waiting for her to build it. All hers. Ron was gone.

And finally, when she opened her eyes, he wept with her.

When they were done, Bryan told Rachel, who had waited outside the door to let them all know that April was fine, and then he slumped into a chair in the corner, too exhausted to move.

Fifty Eight

J ane sat in the motel room on the flowered bedspread that looked as if it belonged in the fifties, trying not to notice the dust and the musty air that poured out of the heater.

She ran her hands through her once blond hair, now a dull gray, trying to decide what to do. She had arrived in Spring Falls in time to hear on the news that the woman had been found and was now recovering in the hospital. Apparently, she had thrown herself out of the car to escape. The man, believed to be her husband, was still missing.

Of course it was her husband, she muttered at the TV. And then berated herself for not being happy for the woman's escape. But she thought she had come to help find the woman, and now what should she do? What could she possibly do that would help them find Ron Page?

You came this far. Keep going, Jane said to herself. *Go to the police and tell them what you know. It could help.*

It would help her anyway. Maybe that was what this visit was all about. A chance to tell the truth, and begin a new life. She had wasted so much of this one running away from what happened instead of facing it.

Jane had seen the police station as she came into town, so she knew where it was. She had also passed the street that led to the small community college. The college where a million years before, she had thought she would go to begin her journey to becoming someone. Someone other than a cheerleader in a town that was barely on the map.

Perhaps when this is all over, I could go there now? Jane wondered. Then laughed at herself. How foolish. She was long past college age, and she didn't know what she wanted to do anymore, anyway.

Jane knew that if she was ever going to find out what she could be in the future, she would have to first tell the truth about the past. She would have to tell someone how she knew Ron Page.

Pushing herself off the bed, she looked at herself in the cracked and graying mirror and tried to smile. She and the mirror belonged together. The mirror couldn't change, but she could.

Get on with it, she said to her reflection.

Fifty Nine

B ooker shouted, "Yes," as he hung up his phone. Addie looked up at him, wondering what all the fuss was about. Booker had brought Addie with him to the station, feeling guilty for neglecting her over the last few days. He expected another long day, and he didn't want to leave her alone again. His next-door neighbor would come over twice a day, but it wasn't the same.

Besides, she was a comfort to everyone in the station. Addie had been an easy dog to train, and he was grateful that he had taken the time to do it. Now she was his rock.

He bent down and scratched her head, saying, "April is fine. Can you believe it? She's hurt, but alive." Addie yawned as if to say she knew it all along.

Booker let himself breathe in relief. When she called, Bree mentioned that the couple from Doveland had helped bring April back. He didn't understand what that meant, but it didn't matter.

Now he could concentrate on one thing, finding Ron Page. But as much as he didn't want it to be true, he was afraid they had lost him.

Based on where they found April, they knew Ron was heading north to Canada, and he already had plenty of time to get there. With the snow, the fog, the slippery roads, and the fact that they didn't know about what kind of car he was driving other than a dark SUV, all pointed to the possibility that he had eluded them.

Booker didn't doubt that once Ron reached Canada, he had a new identity waiting for him. Still, they had to look. Picking up the phone, he contacted his team to alert them to the news.

A few minutes later Nicky walked in his door.

"They don't need me at the hospital," she said. "I was wondering if there was anything I can do here to help."

"You helped, Nicky," Booker said. "Without you, we might never have known. And now that we do, we'll keep looking. And you can start living a life."

"Without Sara," Nicky said.

"She would want you to go on."

Nicky nodded, knowing that to be true, but still not sure what to do with her life, now that the consuming focus of discovering and revealing who had taken her sister was gone.

"But I still don't know what happened to her."

Booker's intercom beeped. "There is a woman out here who says she has information about Ron Page."

"I'll go," Nicky said.

"No, stay. You might be able to help her tell the story."

Nicky nodded and turned to say hello. And froze.

The two women stood looking at each other. Neither moving. Afraid they were wrong. And then they were in each other's arms. Sobbing and laughing at the same time.

"Sara," Nicky said, and Booker smiled for the first time in what felt like days.

Sixty

B ooker told the story of Nicky and Sara's reunion that night at Judith's house. Everyone was there. April, wrapped in blankets, a bandage on her head, looking pale but determined, sat on the couch. Marsha and Cindy flanked her, making sure she had everything she needed.

"Where are Nicky and Sara now?" Bree asked.

"They went back to Jakestown. They said they had some healing to do."

"Do you think we'll see them again?" Judith asked.

"Nicky said they'd be back at some point. They have a lot of years to catch up on first."

No one had to ask why Sara was still alive. Now they knew Ron had escalated from rape to murder after he and April moved to Silver Lake. Where all the bodies of the missing women were, they didn't know. Yet.

They didn't bring up Ron's name either. He had disappeared. And they all knew that they would make sure that he never touched April's life again.

There was only one thing left to do before they could all move on from the horror of what Ron had done. April's children still needed to be told. Since both families lived out of the country, they wouldn't have heard about their father. Booker had done a good job of keeping the story contained, but he couldn't do that for long.

Judith wanted April to tell them now before they heard it from someone else. But April said she couldn't do it. Not today, anyway. So they were leaving it until the morning.

No one expected Ron to contact his children. He had barely noticed them before. Why would he start now? Booker had alerted the authorities about Ron. They would watch for him, just in case he decided to see them.

The Ruby Sisters' focus was not on Ron, they would leave that to others. April and her future were all that was important. It was something they could do something about. And they would.

Bree watched Booker as he talked and wondered if they would ever talk about what had happened back in high school. It seemed petty compared to what had happened between April and Ron. But still. They hadn't resolved it yet.

Besides, it only compounded her worries about how her old feelings about Booker returning. It bothered her. Was it right? And what would Paul say?

"Before we leave," Rachel said, "Bryan has something else he can do for you."

"You've done so much for us already," Judith said. "You brought our friend back."

"My honor," Bryan said, thinking that it was times like this that made him happy for his gift.

He wasn't sure if what else he had to tell them would be taken as well as returning a friend, because this time, he would help them let someone go.

Bree looked at Bryan and started to cry.

"It's Paul, isn't it?"

Bryan nodded. "He's been waiting for this secret about Ron to come out. Waiting for everything to be okay between you and your daughter. He's been helping when he could, but now, he says it's time for him to move on, and he wanted to tell you while your friends surround you."

Looking at Booker, he added, "And Booker."

"No." Bree said. "Not here. Not now."

Bryan waited. "It's not something I can change, Bree. He would like to move on, but he needs you and Booker to be okay."

Booker thought that the world had gone mad. They were all sitting here talking about a dead man as if he were in the room. And he was supposed to tell Bree now about something that had happened when they were teenagers? In front of all her friends?

Maybe that's the point, he thought. *The Ruby Sisters all need to hear it at the same time.*

"I know. It's hard to believe, Booker," April said, shrugging off her blankets. "But it's true. When I was lost by the side of the road, Paul was there with me. He wouldn't let me die. And then Bryan found me and brought me back."

"Can you see Paul now?" Bree asked.

"No. I think that it was only because at the time I was where he is. Now I'm not. But somehow Bryan can be in both places. So it's true Booker, whether you like it or not."

All eyes turned to Booker.

"You've got to be kidding," he said.

When no one spoke, he knew he had no choice. Sitting up straighter, brushing his hair back with his hand, and taking a deep breath, he turned to Bree,

"I'm sorry, Bree. It was so long ago. And now it seems so unimportant. It just grew in importance because I didn't tell you."

When still no one spoke, he continued. "It was my dad. He abused my mother. It got worse while we were in high school. And all I could see was myself being exactly like him. I liked you too much to hurt you. So I ran away."

Bree let out a long sigh. "I'm sorry too, Booker. And as you said, it was a long time ago. Not important now, but I am glad you told me. And I wish you would have told us all then. We might have been able to help."

Marsha nodded, thinking about her home life as a teenager. Yes, she could have helped, and he could have helped her get through her problems, too.

"Geez, what a day," Cindy said after a long silence. "Actually, what a week."

"Yes," Judith agreed. "So many secrets have been told."

"And now we can move on?" Marsha asked, knowing that there was more than one secret that still hadn't been told. But they were hers and she was going to keep them.

"It's what Paul has wanted from all of us, isn't it?" Bree said, wiping away her tears away with a tissue Cindy handed her. "But I don't want Paul to go. Even though I can't see him, I have felt him with me, and it's been such a comfort to believe he was here."

Bryan smiled. "That's the thing Bree. He will always be with you. Just because he is moving on doesn't mean he will leave you. It's hard to explain. But it's true."

"Can you make it so I can see him?"

"Try holding onto Bryan. It usually works for me," Rachel said.

Bryan stood, and all five Ruby Sisters gathered around him. Bruce and Booker looked at each other and then stayed seated. This was not for them.

"May we?" Cindy asked.

Bryan nodded. And then, all of them watched as Paul Stanford Mann, the man the Ruby Sisters knew and loved, moved into the Light. For a moment, the world made sense. A feeling of compassion and love washed over them and stayed as the Light faded. It was a moment none of them would ever forget.

Sixty One

Booker was right. Ron had made it to Canada. But he was wrong in thinking that Ron would never return.

Ron was furious at what April had done. He had driven on, after April threw herself from the car, knowing he couldn't stop. But April was still his wife. Someday he would have to go back and get her.

But not now, he told himself.

Now he needed to disappear. But he was a patient man. He could wait. Even if it took years, he would return for her, and the Ruby Sisters would not be able to stop him.

He was wrong, of course. But Ron, so brilliant about so many things, was blind, as all evil is, to seeing how it would end for him.

Author Note

Thank you for reading this book! I hope you enjoyed it as much as I have loved writing it. I love, love, love writing, but knowing someone else might enjoy the stories in my head makes all the work needed to make a book come into the world worth it a thousand times over.

I believe in the power of community, and friendship, and how together the world can become a place of joy and love. Not to say that there won't be challenges, but if faced together, they become easier, which, of course, is what *The Ruby Sisters* series is about.

The next book in this series will have Marsha as the focus. What's her secret? Does she have only one? What will she do with her life? Here's a hint. In every Ruby Sisters book, there is a mystery and a love story. Read *And Then She Remembered* to find the next one.

And of course, all the other members of this ensemble will live their lives right along with her. Will Ron return in the next book? What will happen between Booker and Bree? Or Judith and Bruce?

You can find more about the series at becalewis.com/books/the-ruby-sisters and sign up for my mailing list to learn more.

Happy Reading! *Beca*

PS:

Did you enjoy meeting Rachel and Bryan? They are visitors from the book series, *Stories From Doveland*. You can read their story in the stand-alone book *In-Between*.

Also By Beca

The Ruby Sisters Series: Women's Lit, Friendship
A Last Gift, After All This Time, And Then She Remembered...

Stories From Doveland: Magical Realism, Friendship
Karass, Pragma, Jatismar, Exousia, Stemma, Paragnosis,
In-Between, Missing, Out Of Nowhere

The Return To Erda Series: Fantasy
Shatterskin, Deadsweep, Abbadon, The Experiment

The Chronicles of Thamon: Fantasy
Banished, Betrayed, Discovered, Wren's Story

The Shift Series: Spiritual Self-Help
Living in Grace: The Shift to Spiritual Perception
The Daily Shift: Daily Lessons From Love To Money
The 4 Essential Questions: Choosing Spiritually Healthy Habits
The 28 Day Shift To Wealth: A Daily Prosperity Plan
The Intent Course: Say Yes To What Moves You

Imagination Mastery: A Workbook For Shifting Your Reality
Right Thinking: A Thoughtful System for Healing
Perception Mastery: Seven Steps To Lasting Change
Blooming Your Life: How To Experience Consistent Happiness

Perception Parables: Very short stories
Love's Silent Sweet Secret: A Fable About Love
Golden Chains And Silver Cords: A Fable About Letting Go

Advice:
A Woman's ABC's of Life: Lessons in Love, Life, and Career from
Those Who Learned The Hard Way
The Daily Nudge: So When Did You First Notice

Acknowledgments

I could never write a book without the help of my friends and my book community. Thank you, Jet Tucker, Jamie Lewis, Barbara Budan, and Diana Cormier for taking the time to do the final reader proof.

You are a loyal and much-loved reader team. You can't imagine how much I appreciate it.

A huge thank you to Laura Moliter for her fantastic book editing.

Thank you to every other member of my Book Community who helps me make so many decisions that help the book be the best book possible.

Thank you to all the people who tell me they love to read these stories. Those random comments from friends and strangers are more valuable than gold.

And as always, thank you to my beloved husband, Del, for being my daily sounding board, for putting up with all my questions, my constant need to want to make things better, and for being the love of my life, in more than just this one lifetime.

Other Places To Find Beca

- Facebook: facebook.com/becalewiscreative

- Instagram: instagram.com/becalewis

- Twitter: twitter.com/becalewis

- LinkedIn: linkedin.com/in/becalewis

- Youtube: www.youtube.com/c/becalewis

About Beca

Beca writes books she hopes will change people's perceptions of themselves and the world, and open possibilities to things and ideas that are waiting to be seen and experienced.

At sixteen, Beca founded her own dance studio. Later, she received a Master's Degree in Dance in Choreography from UCLA and founded the Harbinger Dance Theatre, a multimedia dance company, while continuing to run her dance school.

After graduating—to better support her three children—Beca switched to the sales field, where she worked as an employee and independent contractor to many industries, excelling in each while perfecting and teaching her Shift System® and writing books.

She joined the financial industry in 1983 and became an Associate Vice President of Investments at a major stock brokerage firm, and was a licensed Certified Financial Planner for over twenty years.

This diversity, along with a variety of life challenges, helped fuel the desire to share what she's learned by writing and speaking, hoping it will make a difference in other people's lives.

Beca grew up in State College, PA, with the dream of becoming a dancer and then a writer. She carried that dream forward as she fulfilled a childhood wish by moving to Southern California in 1968. Beca told her family she would never move back to the cold.

After living there for thirty-one years, she met her husband Delbert Lee Piper, Sr., at a retreat in Virginia, and everything changed. They decided to find a place they could call their own, which sent them off traveling around the United States. They lived and worked in a few different places before returning to live in the cold once again near Del's family in a small town in Northeast Ohio, not too far from State College.

When not working and teaching together, they love to visit and play with their combined family of eight children and five grandchildren, read, study, do yoga or taiji, feed birds, and work in their garden.